Prayers Answered by Christmas

BY

AWARD-WINNING AND BESTSELLING AUTHOR

Pat Simmons

Beta reader: Stacey Jefferson
Editor: Chandra Sparks Splond
Proofreader: Judicious Revisions LLC

ISBN- 978-1977905567

ISBN- 1977905560

WHAT READERS ARE SAYING

5 Stars

I love this book, it was a wonderful Christmas story and such a beautiful testament to the spirit and presence of God for what and how he can bring a marriage back together, what God has joined together let no man put asunder; I will definitely share this book with family and friends and others looking for a good Christmas book, good Christian love story, this was a wonderful read, I love the Author she's just the greatest♥--Mary on *Couple by Christmas*

5 Stars

Awesome storyline. I ALWAYS enjoy Pat Simmons books. The storyline is on point and she deals with real life issues. She doesn't compromise her principles as a Christian author and that means a lot.—DRBattenon on *Couple by Christmas.*

5 Stars

"Heartwarming. A wonderful Christian novel about true love. I love the way the author intertwined scriptures into the story."—Angela on *A Baby for Christmas*

5 Stars

"Pat Simmons did it again! This book is full of

love, life lessons and most importantly Christ." — Joyce N. on *A Noelle for Nathan*

5 Stars

"Simmons developed the characters so that I was drawn into their stories. I could feel every emotion." —Donnica Copeland, APOOO BookClub, Sista Talk Book Club, *Not Guilty of Love*

5 Stars

"This book is for everyone who feels there are no second chances in life. I always want to be a better person after reading her books—a better Christian, a better everything. This is truly a must-read book." —Theresa Cartwright Lands on *Crowning Glory*

PROLOGUE

Eight-year-old Mikaela Washington knelt at her bedside. Her younger sister by two years, Alyssa, was already fast asleep in the other twin bed, clutching one of the stuffed animals their Grandma Washington had given them for Christmas.

Folding her hands, Mikaela bowed her head. "Dear Jesus, Happy Birthday! My Sunday school teacher says You had to be born as a baby with a mommy and daddy, so you could die a King and bring us good gifts." She frowned. That didn't make sense. Shrugging, she continued, "Thank you for my presents today from Grandma, auntie, uncles..." She listed everything. "Grandma says I'm to be thankful—and I am, but," she paused, "next Christmas, can I have a new mommy—a good one. She has to be pretty too and like kids. I want—"

"Mikaela," Daddy said from the hallway outside, "time to get in bed."

She opened her eyes and looked over her shoulder. "Okay, Daddy." Turning back, she whispered, "Don't forget, a mommy next Christmas. In Jesus' name. Amen."

CHAPTER ONE

March, three months later...

Marlon Washington scanned the packed banquet room at the Drury Inn in St. Louis for the second wedding anniversary gala. The whoopla was for his younger brother, Derek and his wife, Robyn, who had been divorced, then resolved their differences. They decided to re-marry on the anniversary of their divorce date. At least someone had a happy ending in their life.

At thirty-eight, and the oldest of four boys—two lived out of state—Marlon should have been the one leading by example when it came to marriage—no, that honor should have fallen on their father. Marlon grunted. Tyrone Washington had divorced his mother and was working on marriage number three. Their so-called "male role model" had failed to show his sons what a happy marriage looked like. His church-going mother made peace with her ex after the divorce and urged her sons to do the same. All four of them had, but they weren't strong father-son bonds.

Now, Marlon reigned as the sole second generation divorcee since Derek and Robyn were once again husband and wife. They were the family's success story, so it made sense for them to go overboard on the festivities: live music, food, and colorful decorations.

His heart twisted tighter than a head full of microbraids when he overheard Mikaela praying for another mommy for herself and Alyssa—who barely remembered her mother.

"Hey." He felt a nudge before he blinked. When had Robyn and Derek made their way to him? How long had he been in a daze?

"Why are you being anti-social?" Derek grinned with no cares in the world.

"I'm not. Just thinking." He thought he was doing a good job of being his daughters' "mom" and dad, but Mikaela's prayer revealed he was missing the mark. Marlon folded his arms and shared what was on his mind.

"If that's the case, there are a couple of single sisters that would love to keep you company."

"I'm not interested—not yet anyway."

"Hmm-mm. But it's coming. You may not have caught a garter, but somehow, you did get in the line of fire when I threw my flowers after our courtroom ceremony. Don't think I've forgotten about that," Robyn teased, then laughed. "A man catching the bouquet.'

"Funny." He slipped his hands in his pants pockets, then on second thought loosened the bow tie that all the male guests were asked to wear, not for a wedding, but a celebration of their two year re-marriage anniversary.

"Okay, so you aren't ready to get hitched again, but it could be worse." Derek snickered. "Your eight-year-old could be getting a jump-start on praying for her prince-charming." The couple laughed. Marlon didn't see the humor.

Catching the flowers at their renewal had been a fluke. It had no sentimental value to him. That coveted prize was for the ladies. That's what he got for walking by on the way to escorting Mikaela to the bathroom. Realizing what he had, he passed it to the person beside him who happened to be Mikaela, so he snatched it back.

"She won't be cashing in on that until she's at least forty-something. As for me—" he shrugged—"I thought I was done until I heard that prayer. Maybe I should settle like Dad to get a home-cooked meal every day and a mother who will love my two little girls as her own."

"You don't have to settle, brother-in-law." Robyn had a sober expression. "God has earthly as well as heavenly treasures for us." She cited Third John 2: *Beloved, I wish above all things that thou may prosper and be in health, even as thy soul prospers.* "Stop sending the girls to church with Mother Washington, come with them and see what

God has in store for you," she almost pleaded with him.

"I do come—sometimes," he defended.

"Yeah, at least half a dozen times a year." Derek bobbed his head "Don't think I'm not counting."

Marlon grunted. "No need. I'm sure God is keeping tabs." Guilt kept him away. He might be many things, but he didn't want hypocrite to be among them, and having a hand in the demise of his marriage didn't make him feel like a squeaky clean victim. The only difference was he walked away without a criminal record. Tammy didn't. His ex had four more years to serve. The former Mrs. Marlon Washington was sentenced to eight years in prison for attempted murder—his—when she found out he cheated on her as a retaliation of her cheating on him. That was stupid on his part. The woman had been gorgeous on the outside, but sneaky on the inside. Of course, Marlon didn't know that when he fell hard and married her for love.

With Tammy, Marlon was determined to show his father what a happily-ever-after life looked like. What a joke. Instead, Marlon saw infidelity at its worse. The bottom line was the chick was crazy. After the shooting, he filed for divorce and was awarded custody of his two daughters who reminded him daily that he was the best dad in the world.

"I'm glad you two reconciled, but there isn't any

love lost between me and my ex." He walked away. He needed another drink—Dr. Pepper—on the rocks.

Portia Hunter, the ex-Mrs. Leonard Hunter, stared at her divorce decree papers. "What a waste of my heart," she mumbled.

Until her marriage was dissolved, it had taken numerous late-night phone calls to her mother, tear-soaked pillows and her mother's prayers for recovery before Portia had the strength to utter, "I refuse to let Leonard rob me of happiness." She exhaled. "Lord, do You have a godly man looking to love me?"

"Christ orders our steps, even if the devil steps in our path, sweetie," her mother, Carol always said to encourage her.

"Yep." Portia patted the document on her counter, then gazed out her kitchen window.

The spring blooms bordering her manicured lawn lulled the chaos in her world. How did a man who professed his love one day turn around and burn it to a crisp before they celebrated their second wedding anniversary? What signs did she miss, or ignore that something was wrong? At eighteen, she attended college to prepare for a career; at twenty-nine, she walked down the aisle, preparing to be a lifelong wife and mother. Now, at thirty-three, Portia had no idea what to do with her life.

She knew the devil had planted decoys in the church since the Bible days, but Portia never thought the disguise would be so authentic that she would marry one. She sighed and turned away from the window. She scanned her worldly possessions— what was left after Leonard raided their house for things he took for his new place with... Portia refused to say the adulteress' name.

She didn't care if Leonard had paid for the stuff, Portia had picked it out. After that slap in the face, the next blow came when he had the audacity to run up charges on her credit cards and not make the payments. By the third strike, Portia admitted her marriage was irrevocably broken when Leonard announced their house was no longer his mailing address, so there was no reason to pay his share of the mortgage. Portia did her best to maintain the bills on her salary, but the debt had been too great, and so was the stress.

Although her battle wounds were fresh, Portia was determined to rise from the ashes—someday. Maybe. Why should Leonard be happy and not her?

Portia took her smoothie and swiped her phone off the counter. Relaxing in the family room, which still contained an ottoman, recliner and a small flat screen, she called her mother. Then she added her only sibling, Coy, whose unique name was a combination of their parents' Carol and Roy.

Hopefully, her sister was well rested from working her twelve-hour shifts as a nursing supervisor.

"You sound in good spirits, baby," Carol said after initial greetings, "but I worry about you alone in that big house. You don't even have a dog."

"I have an alarm."

Hmph. "Canines leave a better calling card. I have plenty of room," her mother said from her Dallas condo. Six years ago, her parents had downsized from a house in St. Louis and relocated to a retirement community in Texas. Although her father, Roy, died not long after he escorted Portia down the aisle, her mother stated she could no longer tolerate St. Louis' chilly winters and remained in the South.

Coy Carter lived in a condo in Kirkwood, a suburb in St. Louis County. She was also a divorcee, but not because of another woman. Coy's ex deserted his family—loser. "I know my place isn't as spacious as yours with my two bedrooms, sis, but you're welcome to stay here and regroup—free room and board. Plus, I could use the help juggling work with Emerald's activities." Her eight-year-old niece was a sweetie-pie. Too bad Emerald was an only child.

Gnawing on her lips, Portia considered her options. The bank would foreclose on her house before the end of the year anyway, and she would be forced to find another place to live. "Thanks, sis. I'll let you know."

"No you won't," her mother contradicted her. "We can't keep having this conversation, sweetie. You really don't have any roots in Kansas City. College and church—when you go—don't count. You got until we get off this phone to give me a definite answer."

"It's not that simple. I've worked hard to become the executive producer for *Kansas City Mid-Day* and earn good money to get the ratings."

"But not enough to pay for expenses that were meant for two. St. Louis and Dallas also have stations, remember?" her mother reminded her of the obvious.

"KOXT does have an ABC affiliate sister station in St. Louis, but I don't know if there are any openings."

"I guess you need to expand your reach on LinkedIn," her sister said.

"It's settled," her mother said after a few minutes to Portia's surprise, because nothing was settled in her life at the moment. "Emerald can spend the summer in Dallas with me while Portia moves in with you, Coy."

After the death of her father, her mother would visit Coy and her grandbaby in the summer to help out. Clearly, not anymore. Portia said nothing as they rearranged her life.

For too long Portia had been going through the motions that she was okay, but she wasn't. She had allowed Leonard to continue to control her life from afar. She stopped going to the church they both had attended. Of course, she still prayed, but not faithfully. In all honesty, she was mad at God for letting her marry Leonard.

"Okay, okay, maybe. I feel like I'm taking two steps back. Hopefully, I'll be able to leap four spaces ahead soon. "Coy, looks like you'll have a roommate by summer."

The two cheered as Portia thought, *Take that Leonard Hunter. I'm moving out and moving on. I'll make somebody a good wife. Jerk!*

The first day of June was a bittersweet moment for Portia as she took her final walk through her Kansas City home. Like a contestant's last catwalk across the stage, ending a reign as the pageant winner, she was turning the crown over to the next homeowner to make good memories.

The first two years of her marriage had been blissful, then Leonard removed his mask and revealed the Christian decoy he was. Yes, it was time to say goodbye to the scene of her heartbreak.

What Leonard hadn't taken and she hadn't sold or given away to charities, Portia piled high in her sedan's backseat—mostly her clothes, shoes, and valuables.

A trailer hitched to her bumper contained her favorite recliner, ottoman, desk set and other accents that she would put in storage in St. Louis, because of Coy's limited space. Walking outside, Portia locked the door and got into her car and drove away from the cul-de-sac without looking back.

She already had a tearful goodbye with well-wishing and sympathetic coworkers. On her behalf, the news director had reached out to its sister TV station in St. Louis. They didn't have any vacancies, but would keep her at the top of the list when they did.

Then there were her church friends. After almost a year of being missing in action because of humiliation, Portia made an appearance to say goodbye for good. During her absence, she felt neither God nor her church members had come to her rescue to counsel Leonard to repent and mend his marriage. It was broken, and even God didn't seem interested in fixing it.

Once on I-70 Eastbound, she blasted any "I Will Survive" and other upbeat tunes on the satellite radio for hours until she arrived in St. Louis. The city hadn't been home since she'd left to attend University of Kansas, then she landed her first job in television and worked her way up to an executive producer. From there, she continue to dig her roots in church, relationships, career—she thought she had it all. There was never a reason for her to move back until now.

"Never say never," she mumbled as she followed her GPS to Coy's suburban Kirkwood condo. "Lord, help me to find my way back home to You, the way it used to be," she prayed. When she turned the corner, to Portia's surprise, colorful balloons bounced from ribbons that were tied the curbside mailbox. Parking in front of her sister's place, she took a deep breath. This would be her home for how long?

Her shoe barely kissed the pavement when her mother—visiting from Texas, sister, and niece rushed out the door to greet her with the fanfare of a heroine's welcome. Overwhelmed with love, she bawled like a baby in their arms.

Inside Coy's home, everything looked the same from Portia's last visit. Her sister was a trendy decorator, and soft accents were against white furniture as if she didn't have a child. Coy had two bedrooms and a sofa sleeper for guests, where Portia expected to take residence until Coy pointed to the spacious loft that overlooked the lower level.

Once designated as Emerald's play area, her sister had converted the space to a makeshift bedroom. An oversized blue cushioned chair next to the same shade blue sofa sleeper seen in a hotel suite. Her new sleeping quarters had a leafy floor plant and two colorful room screens to offer plenty of privacy.

"I wanted you to have some privacy despite the open space."

"Wow. Thank you, sis." Portia was touched her sister had gone through so much trouble for her.

"Auntie, I can bring my dolls upstairs so we can play with them, or my video game, or my..." Emerald listed the many possibilities for entertainment.

Coy stopped her. "You're all packed up and going with Granny in the morning to Texas for the summer, remember?"

"Yeah." She grinned. "But you'll still be here with I come back, won't you?" The worry in the child's eyes tugged at Portia.

Unfortunately, probably so, but she put on a happy face. "I think so."

"Come on. I know my baby is tired after the drive," her mother said, "If you're hungry, Emerald helped me prepare salads and burgers."

First, they helped her bring her suitcases in, then gathered around the kitchen table. There seemed to be an unspoken rule that there would be no mention of her failed marriage with Emerald nearby.

Soon they retired to their sleeping quarters.

Their mom slept in Coy's room while her sister got comfortable on the sleeper sofa in the living room. Portia collapsed in the new temporary bedroom loft. If she was still there in three months, her first purchase would be a full size bed. Closing her eyes, Portia yearned for a happy life with or without a husband.

After a few weeks of sending out résumés to St. Louis media without any responses, Portia was losing faith about the whole new beginning thing. She began to second-guess her decision to quit her sixty-thousand-dollar-a-year job. Despite filing bankruptcy, she still had a car note and without working, it would only take her longer to restore her credit worthiness.

While Coy worked long hours, Portia had too much idle time on her hands. She did morning or evening walks, exploring the neighborhood. The solitude was the perfect backdrop to talk to Jesus throughout the day and especially before bed.

"Lord, I know since my divorce, I've second-guessed so many of my decisions, but You've been faithful to me when I was wishy-washy with You. I'm sorry. Please restore everything the devil stole from me, including my strong walk with You. In Jesus' name. Amen."

The next morning, God answered her prayer when she got a call. "Portia, this is Julie Grant for

KSMT. Sorry for taking so long to touch base with you. I still don't have anything full-time..."

Portia's heart plummeted. It was time to step out of her comfort zone. She could do pizza delivery or retail, temp assignments, whichever paid the most, so she had something for now.

"However, if you're willing to work per diem when folks are on vacation, out sick, and any other reasons when we're short-staffed until something comes along—"

"Yes!" She perked up as her heart pumped faster. Scrap delivery driver. She wasn't a fan of pizza anyway.

"Then we could use your producing skills this Saturday and Sunday. That's all I have for now."

After confirming the times and ending the call, Portia screamed, "Yes. Finally, a blessing." She texted Coy the good news. Let's celebrate.

You treat, Portia texted back. I'll eat. LOL.

Early Saturday morning, the two decided to visit the Farmer's Market for fresh fruits and vegetables.

"Ms. Carter! Ms. Carter!" a high-pitched voice sliced through the crowd.

Both she and Coy turned around to see an adorable little girl waving. "Oh." She chuckled. "That's Emerald's best friend. Come on, I'll introduce you." Her sister started heading that way.

"Give me a sec." Portia perused a batch of strawberries, and she wasn't leaving without making her selection. After finishing the transaction, Portia strolled in her sister's direction. As she approached, she overheard Coy say, "Emerald's spending the summer with her grandmother in Dallas, but she'll be back in time for school."

Facing Portia, Coy smiled and introduced a father and his two daughters. "Mikaela, I want you to meet my baby sister Portia. She just moved here from Kansas City."

Portia rolled her eyes. Babies had no cares in the world—she did. Oh, the joys of a warm bottle and an occasional diaper rash. Re-directing her attention, Portia smiled at the girl. "Hi. Aren't you a cutie?"

Mikaela, who had a golden complexion, brown eyes, and two long braids, beamed. She nodded.

"Mikaela, what do you say?" His baritone voice had a rich broadcast quality. If he didn't work in radio or television, he had truly missed his calling. Yet, her eyes didn't stray from the child to another woman's husband. She already had one at the shamefully fine dad, and that one look was enough

"Oh, thank you. I have a baby sister too."

"Me too," the younger sister, Alyssa, who didn't look more than five or six years old, chimed in. She was also adorable with darker facial features.

"Do you have any kids, Ms. Portia? Girls, not

boys." Mikaela added, then scrunched her nose. "They're stupid."

Portia laughed. *My sentiments exactly*. If her father hadn't chastened her, Portia would have lifted her hand for a high five, and shook her head.

"Nice to meet you all." She lowered her voice and turned to her sister. "We better hurry, I do have a job you know." She beamed giddy with excitement.

She had a job, a job, she silently repeated as her soul praised God for this small blessing.

No good thing will I withhold from them who love Me and walk upright before Me, God whispered Psalm 84:11

"I'll tell Emerald I saw you, Mikaela and Alyssa," As they headed toward Coy's car, she shoved Portia. "Did you see Marlon checking you out?"

"I'm not interested in flirting with another woman's husband."

"Girl, he's divorced."

"Welcome to the heartache club," Portia mumbled, then chided herself for not taking another look.

Stunning barely could define Portia's beauty. Marlon made himself blink as not to stare as she and her sister were walking away. "Wow," finally escaped during the short drive to his mother's house nearby in Meacham Park, a hidden historical black neighborhood not far from the Summit Produce Farmers Market.

The affluent City of Kirkwood annexed the community in the early nineties, ending almost one hundred years of independence because the municipality struggled to provide basic services such as sewers and street maintenance to its residents. Some of the houses had been handed down to generations of families, including many blacks, after being purchased from Elzey Meacham in 1892.

Despite the half-a-million-dollar homes swallowing up more of Meacham Park, his mother refused to move.

Marlon and his brother's homes weren't far away. Neither owned million-dollar homes, but they were still pricey. Derek and Robyn had a two-parent income. Marlon was solo on a very good salary as a union electrician, so it was manageable. The sacrifice was worth it because of the exceptional school district. When Coy moved into the district two years ago, their daughters became fast friends, they were the only blacks in their class.

Mikaela's best friend, Emerald, would be a beauty one day like her mother, but Portia, on the other hand...Marlon had to steady his heart, hold his breath, and not blink to capture her beauty. She was so exquisite one would guess her ethnicity—Latina, Nigerian, or bi-racial. Although the sisters resembled one another, Portia's features were one of a kind.

While she didn't seemed fazed by his presence, Marlon was blown away instantly by hers as he performed a quick, but thorough assessment. Dressed down in casual attire of fashionable jeans with precise rips at her knees, a tank top, and simple tennis shoes, she was just that stunning with her wavy wind-blown hair as if she was about to be the headliner for a photo shoot.

Stylish sunglasses shielded her eyes, but Marlon suspected they were mesmerizing too. His first and only impression about Portia was she wasn't a flirtatious male chaser, like his ex-wife had been, but he had been Tammy's willing victim. Every woman since his divorce seemed to be chasing him, which only made Marlon fall down and play dead. The brief encounter with Portia had the opposite effect. He wanted to know more about her: children, married, a boyfriend?

"Isn't Ms. Portia pretty like my dolls, Daddy?" Mikaela asked from the backseat as if his thoughts were scribbled across a chalkboard.

Where Mikaela was a chatterbox and outgoing, his younger daughter, Alyssa, was quiet and shy, and loved mimicking her big sister.

"She's as pretty as you, Mimi," he replied, using

one of the many nicknames he had given her. She giggled.

Marlon didn't know her story, and she didn't know his. Maybe it was best to leave well-enough alone. *Maybe.*

A few weeks later, Mikaela had enough of these ladies trying to flirt with her daddy while he was watching her turn at bat during her softball game. Miss Tina had bad breath anyway. That night while on her knees praying, Mikaela thanked God for all her relatives, even her mommy in jail. Then she reminded Jesus about her Christmas request. "What about Ms. Portia? She's pretty," Mikaela paused, "but she doesn't have any kids. I hope she likes little girls." She twisted her lips. "Anyway, please forgive me when I was bad and other sins I forgot about. I love You, Jesus. Amen. Good night."

CHAPTER TWO

When Portia's mother returned with Emerald a week before the start of school, Portia couldn't believe she had spent her entire summer working long hours at the television station. She had no complaints.

Seconds after her niece crossed the threshold, the house came alive with Emerald's chatter. "Mommy, did you miss me?" Her niece's tanned face waited expectantly.

Coy hugged her daughter tight. "Every day."

After the long road trip, her mother seemed to purr as she sunk into the sofa. Kicking off her sandals, she wiggled her toes, which had the same nail polish as Emerald's.

Concerned about her safety, Portia offered to drive back to Texas with her, since her hours at work had slowed.

"I'll fly you back, dear," her mother said, offering to cover the plane ticket.

Portia didn't bother arguing. Although she was building her savings again, come the week after Labor Day when all the employees were back, Portia would be begging for hours. During the down time, Portia could spend time with Emerald.

A couple of days later, Portia enjoyed her one-on-one time with her mother on the drive back to

Texas. She was behind the wheel and planned to make the ten-hour drive in one day, not the two it had taken her mother.

"I'm glad you're away from Kansas City."

"Me too." Portia glanced in the rearview mirror before changing lanes. "Although Coy and I worked a lot, when we were at home, we had long talks about love found, lost, marriage, divorce, and children."

"I hope she didn't convince you never to give love another chance. That girl." Her mother shook her head. "She acts like she's content being a single mom, but my grandbaby needs a male role model in her life, whether it's her deadbeat dad or a stepfather, not to mention a brother or sister."

"Mom, Daddy was a good guy—father and husband. You can't imagine the hurt from a bad marriage. Coy and I weren't that lucky." While Portia wore her heartache on her sleeve, depending on her mood, Coy put on a fearless face in front of Portia and her mother, but she and her sister both wanted a happily ever after like their parents.

"Yet," her mother corrected. "Don't give up on love."

"Okay." Portia nodded. "Both men got in our hearts and head. Eric was Coy's childhood sweetheart, so she thought she knew him. Leonard was a church brother, who I thought I knew." She shrugged. "At least Coy has Emerald. I wonder if I'll ever have another chance for a mini-me. How will I know if I've got the right one?"

"Sweetie, detours in life should bring us closer to Jesus. Leonard was a detour. Get back on the path to God, and you'll reach your destination in life and death."

"I know, Momma. I thought I was getting back on track when I came back home and then I started working so many hours that my body craved sleep more than food," she said quietly, guilty of tiptoeing away from God after Leonard performed a speed walk into adultery. "I kinda felt the Lord betrayed me by not saving my marriage."

Every good and perfect gift comes from me. God whispered James 1:17.

In hindsight, Portia concurred Leonard wasn't a gift. She questioned what drew her to Leonard— good-looking, check; successful, check; and godly...a bold no. If God had told her Leonard wasn't the one, she would have played deaf and married him anyway. Her misguided will cost her pride, sanity, and materialistic possessions. "It's time that I restore my relationship with God first."

"It starts with repentance..." Carol held up her hand to stop Portia from interrupting. "I know we say we repent about things, but a lot of times that a surface confession. You need to dig deep in your soul for a spiritual cleansing that only God can give," she finished her say and looked out the window. "My grandbaby sure loved going to church with me. I know Coy working on Sundays prevents her from going sometimes, but you take Emerald when you can. When you can't, read your Bible. Amen?" She faced Portia again.

"Amen," Portia conceded. Music from the radio filled the lull as they retreated to their own thoughts until Portia confessed, "I did a lot of self-reflection while waiting for my divorce to be finalized. I was in love with him, but I'm ashamed to say I had some lust mixed in too. A single brother in the church is a hot ticket." She checked the rearview mirror before changing lanes. "I'm reaping."

Carol reached over and patted Portia's arm. "Don't beat yourself up. Your ex did enough of that on your heart."

"I know, you're right." She bobbed her head.

"Save those dreams for the right man."

Portia mustered a smile for her mother. She was determined not to lose hope in a happily after ever for herself, especially when Leonard taunted her on the day their divorce was granted that he had found "real happiness" with his mistress.

They stopped a couple of times to stretch, ate, then were back on the road, arriving safely in Dallas before dark. After a few days' rest, Portia gave her mother a hug goodbye at DFW Airport.

"I was hoping you could spend an entire week with me." Her mother pouted.

"Can't. I'm Coy's mommy backup."

As she had suspected, when Labor Day hit, the calls for work took a dip, and she picked up her Bible again, but it didn't seem like the Scriptures were saturating her soul. "Lord, help me. It seems harder to find that hiding place in You."

Have faith that I will help you to move on, God whispered, *I'm a rewarder to those who diligently seek Me.*

Portia's eyes teared, thankful that God had spoken to her spirit and directed her to Hebrews 11.

Soon, Portia's surrogate mother duties kicked in when Coy had to go into the hospital when two nurses called in sick. She could see the agonizing of choosing. "Go, sis. I'll take Emerald to the open house at school."

Coy exhaled with relief, then frowned. "You sure?"

"Yes. I got this. Now, go." Portia shooed her out the door, then grabbed her own purse and left with her niece. Once they arrived at Baxter Elementary School, Portia was flooded with childhood memories as they followed directions to the auditorium. Portia had loved school and excelled in her studies from grade school throughout college, thanks to her love of reading that began in kindergarten.

Holding Emerald's hand, she imagined that she was taking her own daughter to school. Locating empty space on the bleachers, the two made themselves comfortable as the principal began promptly with instructions for the school year. Mrs. Torres introduced the staff, which prompted Emerald to point.

"Mrs. Becton's my teacher, Auntie," She stated and bounced in her seat.

Portia shushed her niece and chuckled at her excitement.

"I have packets of forms that parents are required to sign and return, including permission slips for field trips. In your folders, there is a hard copy of the school calendar of events, which lists parent-teacher conferences. All this information is assessable on the school's website…" the principal rambled on.

Stifling a yawn, Portia thought being a parent wasn't all it was cracked up to be. Finally, the meeting was adjourned and guests were invited to have refreshments, visit the classrooms and meet their child's teacher.

Standing from their perch on the benches, Emerald tugged on Portia's arm. "That's my best friend, Mikaela."

Glancing in the direction Emerald was facing,

Portia saw the girl she had met earlier in the summer. "Yes, I know…"

When Mikaela saw Emerald, the girls screamed and raced toward each other. They hugged as if they hadn't seen each other hours earlier in class. The adults, including Portia, were in awe of their affection.

Once the classmates separated, her niece was a chatterbox. "This is my Auntie Portia. She's was living in Kansas City, but she's staying with Mommy and me, because she's d-vorced."

Embarrassed, Portia withheld her groan. She would have to speak to her niece about protocol on how to introduce Portia to her friends. She squeezed Emerald's shoulder to hush her.

A woman shorter than Portia's five-six statue stepped forward. "Hi. I'm Robyn Washington, Mikaela's aunt." She introduced her husband who was holding an adorable little girl and her son who took off when he saw a classmate.

Marlon, Mikaela's father, who she had met briefly, greeted her with a simple hello. That deep voice drew her in. This time, she took a few moments to admire his assets beside the voice. Tall, built, and extremely good-looking.

Before she could engage in adult conversation, her niece disappeared from her side. Working in a newsroom had Portia aware of criminal activity. She knew all about child abductions in public places, so she excused herself and went in search of Emerald who had made her way to the refreshments table. Robyn fell in step with her. "So you're new to the city?"

"I'm originally from here," Portia said, with her eyes locked on Emerald, "but I haven't lived here in fifteen years. Like my niece broadcasted, I'm recently divorced, so I needed a fresh start. I'm working at KSMT-TV." There was a warm vibe about Robyn's personality that seemed genuine. Portia figured she might as well get to know her since their nieces were best friends.

"I don't work far from there. Girl, we've got to have lunch. I know all about divorce. We can swap stories. " She snickered, handed Portia a card with her number. "I better get back to my family. I hope we can get a chance to be friends."

With Emerald in sight, Portia discreetly watched Robyn's interaction with her husband. The woman glowed like a newlywed. She definitely wanted to know how Robyn bounced back and found bliss after all after her divorce.

After being homebound for a week, Portia finally got some hours at the station. Remembering that Robyn worked nearby, she called her.

"Hey, stranger." After telling Robyn she was working, the woman said, "There's this yummy place on Jefferson that has great subs and salads."

"Sounds good." Portia scribbled the directions. "See you right after our noon broadcast." After disconnecting, she smiled. Friends, family, and a job. The completion.

You'll never be complete or satisfied without Me, God whispered.

Portia blinked, busted. Although she had stepped up her Bible reading, she hadn't made much effort to attend church as she had promised her mother. When the newscast had ended, she walked out of the control room, grabbed her purse and left for lunch.

Robyn had already arrived at the cozy café and greeted her with a hug like an old girlfriend. "Nice outfit."

"Thanks." They strolled to the counter, perused the overhead menu board, and placed their orders.

"So, I'm glad we have a chance to get to know each other without the children." Robyn chatted until they received their food trays, then they chose a table in the restaurant, which was halfway occupied.

Robyn gave thanks for their food, then Portia stabbed at her salad filled with salami, peppers, cheese, and other garnishes. She nodded her head, then dabbed at her mouth. "I'm mommy backup."

Portia smiled. "It's nice to be involved in Emerald's life, in case I never have any children of my own."

Robyn frowned. "Just because you're divorced, you shouldn't give up on a family," she said matter-of-fact. "Derek and I were divorced."

Portia almost choked on the lettuce. She coughed to clear her airway.

"You okay?" Robyn stood, ready to assist.

Portia waved her off. After a few sips of water, she was able to regulate her breathing. "You remarried your ex?" She shook her head in disbelief. "That must have been for twenty-four hours, because truly that man loves you."

"And I love that hunk back, but we were divorced for two years. We're a product of God's restoration. We took the easy way out of our marriage when the going got tough. Is there any chance you and your ex could reconcile?"

"A capital N-O, but I'm glad you had a happy ending." Portia resumed eating.

"You sound like my brother-in-law. There was no love lost between him and Tammy." She paused. "Well, his story isn't mine to tell."

She briefly wondered, what *was* his story? Didn't matter really. No two divorces were alike, she thought. "Leonard and I will never get back together, unless I'm okay with an open marriage, and I'm not. He left me for another woman." She shivered at the thought of sharing the bed with a man who had another woman's scent on him. "I was angry, devastated, humiliated, and..." She stopped, not wanting to use anymore brain power on Leonard.

"Sounds like he was a parasite, trying to suck the life out of you. *Hmph.*" Robyn jutted her chin.

"Exactly." The woman had called it right. "In January, I'll be officially single for one year. I plan to keep moving forward and not looking back."

Tilting her head, Robyn seemed to study her, then smiled. "Let me invite you to my church. God will hide you in His secret place until the right man comes along."

No more excuses. "After the wrong one, I have to believe there is a 'right' one out there. There has to be," Portia said more to convince herself. "I'm not sure about Coy, but I'm not working Sunday, so Emerald and I will be there. Text me the address and time."

CHAPTER THREE

Marlon strolled into his mother's house where his daughters waited for him after school. Robyn was there, too, to pick up her son and daughter.

"Portia and I had lunch today."

His interest piqued, overhearing the conversation his sister-in-law was having with his mother.

"That's Mikaela's best friend's aunt, right?" Lane Washington queried.

"Yep. She's sweet, and I really liked her, but—"

"Daddy!" Mikaela screamed, racing toward him with her arms open. Alyssa was on her heels.

But what? Marlon wanted to know, but all conversation ceased as he became the center of attention. Chuckling, he squatted to receive his daughters' hugs. Marlon always wanted to be their hero. Standing, he lifted each girl in his arms, then smacked noisy kisses on their cheeks as they giggled.

Robyn's children wanted in on the fun. "Hi, Uncle Marlon," his nephew said.

After releasing the girls, he rubbed Tyler's head and tickled Deborah's belly.

Next he greeted the women with kisses to their cheeks. "I heard you had lunch with Portia. What's her story? I was thinking about…" any other time he would never state his intentions about a woman in front of his mother and sister-in-law, but if Robyn and Portia were becoming friends, maybe his sister-in-law could feel the woman out about compatibility, "inviting her to dinner."

Instead of her being delighted at his interest, Robyn shook her head. "Back off, brother-in-law."

"Back off says the woman who has been praying for me to move on?" Marlon thought she was kidding, so he turned his attention to the pots on the stove.

"Can I go, too, Daddy?" Mikaela asked, reminding them of her presence.

"Me too," Alyssa chimed in.

"Stay out of grown folks' conversations." His mother shooed her grandchildren from the kitchen.

Marlon washed his hands, grabbed a plate, and helped himself to whatever his mother had prepared, then sat next to his sister-in-law. "Why can't we be friends?"

"As pretty as Portia is, no man with regulated hormone levels would want to be *just* friends with her," Robyn said. "Her divorce crushed her. I think she's still got some healing to do. You've been there, done that, and moved on," she added softly.

Some days if the devil didn't taunt him with guilt.

"God bless her," his mother whispered, shaking

her head. "I'll be praying God gives her a new heart. I've waved at her a few times when I've picked up the girls and she was there for Emerald."

"I invited her to our service on Sunday." Robyn lifted a brow as if a challenge. "Maybe you should stop being a guest and bring your *own* daughters to church." Standing, she patted his shoulder, kissed his mother, and gathered her children to leave. "Time to go, Tyler and DeeDee."

Once they were alone, he casually said, "You know, Mom, I think I can adjust my hours, so I can pick up the girls from school."

"Okay," she said from her spot at the sink without looking his way. "Let me know what day."

"What day does Portia pick up Emerald?" He smirked to himself.

Lane chuckled. "This is only the second week of school, so any day Monday through Friday."

"You're not going to be more specific, huh?"

She turned around and cast him a somber expression, "I know all about divorce, remember? Everyone doesn't process it the same way. I remember how crushed you were. Robyn thinks Portia needs to heal emotionally. You'll be able to tell when she's ready." Lane squinted. "Keep your eyes open."

There was something about that woman that piqued his interest, and it wasn't just her looks. It sounded as if they had kindred spirits when it came to broken vows. "Noted."

The next day at work, Marlon's foreman granted him approval to adjust his schedule, so he could pick up his girls after school twice a week. His boss was a firm supporter of fathers being active in their children's lives. Marlon didn't add the tidbit that he was trying to keep his eyes on a certain lady. Wednesdays and Thursdays were his assigned early days, and Marlon hoped Portia would be on carpool duty.

She wasn't. Coy picked up Emerald, so Marlon activated Plan B. Sunday morning, he chuckled to himself. Marlon thought there was something about Portia herself, pulling at his heartstrings. Maybe, it was God using her to draw him back to Him.

Have you not heard I am *a jealous God? What do I get?* God whispered. The reprimand forced him into a moment of reflection.

I'm looking for a clean heart, God continued his chastening.

"Please forgive me, Lord. Although I thank You for the beautiful bait, I plan to be at church on Sundays from here out. He couldn't remember receiving so many hugs and kisses from his daughters when he told them he was taking them to church, and they didn't have to go with their grandma.

Marlon could manage Mikaela and Alyssa's hair with the basic braids, twists, oil scalps, and even detangling it after shampoos. His oldest took over the reins recently, informing him she was old enough and smart enough for bathing and dressing herself and her sister. As long as the colors looked okay together, Marlon signed off on it.

Mikaela had an adorable smile with a mischievous streak. To say she was a daddy's girl was an understatement. Even though Tammy's imprisonment tore his family apart, Mikaela seemed to bounce back first. She tried to take her mother's place in the kitchen. Most times, it was a disaster, but with a little coaching by her grandma, she became a pro with instant breakfasts, sandwiches, and basic salads. In addition to book sense, she seemed wise beyond her years. When he overheard her asking God for a mommy, that's when he faced the truth that Tammy had left a void in his daughters' lives.

Alyssa was shy and had no problem letting Mikaela take the lead. His baby girl was content with a book over a video game. Both girls were beauties. Where Alyssa had his medium brown skin tone, Mikaela had a light golden hue like...instead of Tammy coming to mind, Portia's image became crisp before his eyes.

When he was ready, Marlon inspected the girls,

then ushered them to the backseat of the car. After entering Holy Ghost Temple, Marlon refused to let his attention stray to search out Portia. She wasn't the keeper of his soul.

After the choir sung and a couple of announcements, Pastor Kinder stood at the podium. "A soul is a precious gift to lose," he began, touching the screen on his tablet. "The book of Mark, chapter eight and verse thirty-six reads *for what shall it profit a man, if he shall gain the whole world, and lose his own soul?'* Only you can answer that. What lust—and it isn't always sexual immortally—has overpowered your common sense that you're willing to take a risk at missing heaven?"

Marlon squirmed in his seat. The message was for him! Had God been sitting on this sermon waiting for him to show up? Although he didn't consider himself lusting after Portia, he was interested in her—very. Pastor Kinder continued to throw out questions while Marlon underwent self-examinations.

"Daddy, there's Emerald?" Mikaela said, patting him on his shoulder moments after the benediction.

Before the sermon, he would have led the way to his daughter's friend. Now, he realized his spiritual life had to have priority over his desire for a social calendar.

"Can I go speak to her?"

"Sure." Taking Alyssa's hand, his other daughter stayed at his side as they trailed Mikaela. *Tread careful,* he coaxed himself when he joined Robyn, Coy, Portia and the three girls. God hadn't revealed Portia's purpose in his life. Would He?

CHAPTER FOUR

Portia welcomed her new monthly routine. Coy would enjoy breakfast with Emerald, drop her off at school then head to Des Peres Hospital for her twelve-hour shift—sometimes more. When the station did put Portia on the schedule, it was early mornings, which allowed her to pick up Emerald.

But those jobs kept them both away from church since their first visit to Robyn's. Still the message lingered and Portia didn't miss her time with the Lord, even if she had to go inside the ladies' room and pray quietly and meditate on a scripture from her online Bible.

No matter what Scriptures throughout the day, or at night, she often stumbled upon Jeremiah 29:11 always resurfaced: *For I know the thoughts that I think toward you, says the LORD. Thoughts of peace, and not of evil, to give you an expected end.* And she always asked, "Then why did You let my marriage end?"

She had reread that passage during the early days of discourse in her marriage. Believing God, she was waiting for that expected good outcome in her life.

One day at work, she was pondering a deeper understanding when Mikaela's aunt called her. "Hey, stranger. If you're working today, let's do lunch."

"Your timing is perfect, Robyn, because I've been working four days in a row."

"How about TGI Fridays?"

"Sure, I'll treat for burgers," Portia said and disconnected. An hour later, she was perusing the menu when Robyn rushed into the restaurant and greeted her with a hug,

Once they were seated, and soft drinks were ordered, Robyn leaned back. "So how's everything going? I haven't seen you at church," she said with a concerned expression.

"I've been working. Although I'm not money hungry, I'm trying to get on full-time, and saying no to work doesn't plead my case," she explained. "That message inspired me to stay focused on my spiritual growth, so I really can't wait to come back." Portia beamed.

"Amen," Robyn interjected as their server asked for their selections. They decided on burgers and fries, then Robyn continued, "Now, I may be married, but I do believe in a girl's night out, so let's get together whenever you have an evening off and it can be any day through the week." She was hyped. "My husband can babysit and I know Marlon will be okay watching the girls, if Coy wants to tag along too."

"I've never known a man who enjoys or feels competent to watch their children." Portia giggled.

"The Washington men pass the test. Marlon can even comb hair. Derek better be glad our daughter still has short, curly hair."

Portia rested her elbow on the table, then tucked her chin on her hand. So many emotions ran through her head: From *Some women are so blessed,* to *I wish I had married someone like that* to *Face it, I blew my chance.*

"What?" Robyn gave her an odd expression.

Was she thinking out loud? Portia looked away, then shook her head before facing her again. "I want to trust again to fall in love and have a man who loves God, his wife, and his family." She sighed. "Right now, it's far away dream."

"Pray, and I'll pray with you that the Lord Jesus will send the right man to make your dreams come true."

"I guess I better pray that I don't chase away that right man." Portia cleared her throat. "Enough talk about relationships." She changed the subject, and jumped from fashion to hobbies, and they even shared a few Biblical insights until their food arrived.

When Portia and Coy somehow found themselves at home together for a few hours, only because her sister was working a later shift. Coy made a confession. "I feel guilty."

"Huh?" Portia stopped unloading the dishwasher

and stared at her sister, waiting for an explanation.

"Don't get me wrong," Coy hurried to say. "I'm really glad you're here, not because you're helping with Emerald, which I can't thank you enough for helping with homework, picking her up from school and more." She paused, then came to stand by Portia. "I think you'll heal faster away from places in Kansas City that could trigger bad memories, but I just I hope I'm not overwhelming you with Emerald."

Portia playfully bumped her sister. "Staying busy is good for me, and did you forget I'm staying here free, and I feel guilty for that."

"Okay, no pity party." Coy laughed and waved her hands in the air as if she was shaking off bad vibes. "I'm thinking about doing a pajama party this weekend—the three of us." She shrugged. "Something fun to do with my baby."

"Love it." Portia reminisced about the pj parties they had as little girls.

Her niece was beyond excited when Coy told her, and Emerald counted down the days to the weekend. On Friday, when Portia arrived at school for Emerald, her niece's face had an unmistakable glow as she raced toward Portia with her backpack bouncing behind her.

"Is it time for the party, yet, Auntie?" Her eyes sparkled with anticipation.

Portia tapped her nose. "Almost. Your mom is at home getting things ready now."

"Yes!" Emerald hopped on one leg. then the other. Marlon and his daughters were nearby and she felt a fluttering in her heart, or maybe it was a kindred spirit.

Emerald looped her arm through Mikaela's and dragged her toward Portia. "Do you think Mikaela can spend the night too?"

Ambushed, Portia was tongue-tied. Coy was looking forward to some one-on-one fun with her daughter. "We'll have to ask permission."

"Granted," the deep voice of Marlon said from behind her.

She shivered at his deep voice. His muscles bulged in his company-issued uniform, which bared the name of the local utility company. Portia hoped she wasn't drooling. Blinking, she met his eyes. When did they become so hypnotic? "Ah, ah…" She lost her train of thought, then got it back. "I'm talking about my sister. Can you give me a sec?" She walked a few feet away for privacy and called Coy. "Hey, we have a situation."

"What's wrong with my baby?" Panic filled her voice.

"Emerald is fine. She wants to know if Mikaela can come to the party."

"Oh." Coy exhaled into the phone. "Girl, you

scared me. Stop talking media lingo. Of course. It's all about Emerald this weekend. We can't leave Alyssa out. I'm sure she'll want to be with her big sister. Hey, we can handle three little girls."

"Yep, you and I had sleepovers with double that number. I'll tell Marlon it's a go." She disconnected and whirled around. He seemed to follow her every move. "It's a go. Coy says Alyssa is welcomed too."

The girls screamed their delight and formed a group hug.

"Thanks for letting my girls invade your party."

He had dimples too? Portia swallowed. She had a crush on Jimmy Rogers in third grade who had dimples. "Sure. See you in a few."

She almost raced to the car with Emerald. Her hormones were out of whack. Too many romance movies for her.

The scent of Portia's faint perfume clung to Marlon's nostrils. His excitement to see her again matched his daughters' for the pajama party.

"Make sure you pack your toothbrush and clean underwear," he instructed Mikaela.

"I know, Daddy."

While they were busy, Marlon showered, shaved, and primped. Instead of jeans and a worn T-shirt, he upgraded to slacks and a polo.

When he finished, his daughters were sitting on the sofa, swinging their legs. Their kiddie suitcases rested beside them. Judging from their folded arms, they were waiting impatiently for him.

"Come on, Daddy. We're going to be late," Mikaela demanded.

Alyssa nodded and scooted off the sofa, and stood, reaching out for a hug. "You smell good," his baby girl noted.

"Thanks, my lovelies." He engulfed them in a group embrace and smacked loud kisses on their cheeks, then took their mini suitcases. It was important to him to pamper them and show them what to expect from the opposite sex, whether they were eight or eighteen or twenty-eight years old.

In the car, he double-checked that they were strapped in their booster seats. The last time he had been at Coy's house had been a year ago for Emerald's birthday party.

In no time, Marlon parked in front of the immaculate condo, gathered the girls' things, then followed them to the porch. Portia answered the door seconds after he knocked, then Coy appeared at her side. His darlings gave a quick greeting and squeezed between them in search of their friend.

"Sorry," he apologized. "They know better."

"They're excited and so is Emerald. They're fine," Coy argued in their defense. Although

Emerald and Mikaela were in the same grade, Emerald embraced Alyssa as a best friend too.

Standing side by side, both sisters were very attractive, but Portia—wow—she had a double portion of beauty.

"Well, in that case, your guests have arrived." He grinned with a slight bow.

"I'll take those, Marlon. This is an official all-girls zone." Coy smiled and reached for the suitcases. "You can pick them up any time tomorrow afternoon. You're free to enjoy your evening." She politely dismissed him.

Portia said nothing, but her eyes held amusement. Marlon strolled to his car as Coy was closing the door. Whether she intended for him to hear her or not, he chuckled when she said, "That brother has some serious swagger going on."

"Yep, and he smelled good too," Portia replied.

Smirking, it took all of Marlon's willpower not to turn around and acknowledge their remarks. Instead, he slid behind the wheel and drove away a happy man, detouring to his brother's house.

"What's up, brother-in-law?" Robyn opened the door.

Tyler and Deborah were looking up at him, waiting for his attention. Scooping up his niece in his arms, he smothered a kiss on her cheek, then exchanged a fist bump with his nephew. "Can your husband come out and play?" he teased.

"Maybe, where are the girls?" Robyn craned her neck to look behind him.

"They're at Emerald's house for a sleepover."

Robyn twisted her lips and squinted. Whatever was on her mind, she didn't share.

"So, can Derek get a pass for a night out with his big brother, or are you going to keep him in bondage?"

She led him back to the family room where Derek was engrossed in a Cardinals playoff game on TV. "My husband happens to like to be in bondage with his favorite wife."

"You're my only wife," he murmured without looking away from the game.

"Just testing, babe. Good answer."

At a commercial break, Derek finally acknowledged him. "What's up, bro?"

"I was hoping you and I can have some bonding time. The girls are at a sleepover."

"Yeah. I heard." He winked. "I've learned how to multitask thanks to my wife." He reached for Robyn and they shared a brief kiss.

"Hey, not in front of a divorced man," Marlon feigned protest.

"Babe, if you want to hang out, go ahead," she said in a low voice, "but please take your son with you to keep you out of trouble."

Tyler's eyes got wide. "Can we ride go-carts?"

Robyn and Derek groaned. Go-carts seemed to be his nephew's latest craze.

Twenty minutes later, with Tyler in tow, Marlon drove to the indoor and outdoor tracks at the Game Spot. Seconds after Derek purchased their tickets, his nephew was climbing in a go-cart.

"You riding, Dad?" Tyler yelled from his blue car.

"The next round, buddy," he barely got out before his son sped off, then he turned to Marlon. "So, how is Ms. Portia? I know my wife told you to back off, but I know you too well to believe you listened."

"True." Marlon grunted and leaned on the rail to watch his nephew go fast and furious. "She's an attractive woman, and I'm attracted. All I need is five minutes to convince her that I'm a good guy." He paused. "I've held back since hearing the sermon on what profits a man."

Derek was quiet, but waved at Tyler. "That's a good focus. Without the Lord's intervention, there's no way Robyn and I could've reconciled. Has Portia given you any indication that she's interested?"

"I have it on good authority that I have swag and smell good." He grinned.

"Hey, I gave you the tip on the cologne." Derek elbowed him. "Seriously, I'm glad to see you returning to your first love. Jesus is awesome," he said, referencing Revelation 2:4–5: *Nevertheless I have somewhat against thee, because thou hast left thy first love. Remember therefore from whence thou art fallen, and repent, and do the first works; or else I will come unto thee quickly, and will remove thy candlestick out of his place, except thou repent.*

"I know you were messed up after your divorce. I was too. It's good to see you claiming a spot on the pew every Sunday." Derek extended his hand for a shake.

"Me too," Marlon admitted, accepting his hand. For so long, I felt like a hypocrite going to church when I know I didn't have a squeaky-clean record in our marriage."

"Mom always said guilt is the devil's best revenge when we come to Christ. You know what led to those circumstances. Of course, what you did was stupid, but you've repented and moved on. Don't take guilt with you everywhere you go."

Guilt is the devil's best revenge, was another one of Momma's crumbs of wisdom. "Your ex-wife might be in jail, but Christ died to set the captives free—inside and outside prison walls," he mumbled to himself.

"Dad, Uncle Marlon! C'mon," Tyler's voice echoed as he zoomed by them.

They laughed. "I wish I had a son. Don't get me

wrong, I love my girls, but every man needs a son."

"Trust me, any woman out here would be more than willing to carry your son, but be careful next time. She's got to want a family. Tammy wanted a lifestyle. Now, after you, old man." Derek opened the gate to the track. Minutes later, they squeezed their bulky frames into go-carts.

Marlon and Derek relived their childhood in the go-carts until Tyler wore himself out. They decided to call it a night.

"What a workout." Marlon felt like he had been at the gym. "Let's do it again, bro," he said, dropping Derek and Tyler at home.

"Now what?" Marlon mumbled to himself. He wasn't ready to call it a night. Thank God for his little girls, or his life would be as empty as his house without them tonight. Once there, he headed for the shower. As he stepped out, his cell rang. It was almost eleven. That was not a good sign. He hurried to answer.

"Marlon, this is Coy. Nothing serious, but I wanted you to know Alyssa has been throwing up. It could be something she ate, but I don't think she needs a visit to the emergen—"

"I'm on my way," he cut her off. Grabbing his keys, he almost tripped running to the garage until he realized he needed to put on some clothes. Once he had, he jumped behind the wheel of his car. He didn't care if Coy was a nurse or not. When his girls got sick, they were his responsibility.

His heart pounded as he drove to the other side of Kirkwood. He barely parked and turned off the ignition before he was out of the car. He jogged up the short path to the front door, which opened before he could knock.

The sense of urgency he felt seconds ago evaporated at the sight of Portia in cartoon pajamas under an ugly robe. She wore colorful face paint. Her mass of wavy hair was combed into several ponytails. On someone else, her getup would look crazy. Not Portia Hunter, she looked playful and somehow alluring.

"We didn't mean to alarm you." She stepped backed, and Marlon entered.

Too late, he kept to himself and searched the room. "Where is my little girl?"

Portia pointed to the couch where his daughter was balled up. He spied movement in the upper loft. Mikaela peeked from behind a colorful screen and waved. She wore face paint too. She was still up? Music played in the background and the television was on.

Coy hurried downstairs dressed similar to Portia, looking apologetic. "Marlon. I didn't mean for you to come over this time of night. She's not running a temperature and felt better after emptying her stomach, but as her daddy, I wanted you to know."

Her words faded as he stood over Alyssa. He scooped her up in his arms, rubbed his cheek against her cool forehead, then kissed her head. No temp as Coy had said. He exhaled.

Alyssa's lids fluttered open as she gave him a faint smile. "I want to stay, Daddy."

He balked. "No, baby. Daddy's taking you home."

She began to whimper. "I promise I won't throw up no more."

"She's welcome to stay, but it's your call," Coy interrupted. "Ally was able to hold down clear soda and crackers. Some tummies aren't made for junk food overload, and we've had pizza, punch, chips and dip…"

"If it was pepperoni pizza, it was probably too greasy." Marlon frowned. His daughter knew better.

"Come on, Mom, we're waiting for you," Emerald yelled from the loft.

"Just a minute, girls," she hushed. "I can pack her things, if you want."

Although Alyssa's eyes were closed, she shook her head against his chest. He huffed as Coy headed toward the stairs.

Marlon faced Portia. Compassion filled her eyes.

"I really don't know what to do," he told her while snuggling Alyssa.

"Wait a while. When I was a little girl, I never wanted to be separated from my big sissy." She looked at Alyssa. "She's beautiful, such a sweetheart, and a voracious reader. While the other two played, Alyssa and I read in the dark with a flashlight. She got a kick out of that." Her eyes brightened, indicating his daughter wasn't the only one who was enjoying herself. Marlon smiled.

"She was fascinated with *The Princess and the Frog*." Portia reached over and lovingly stroked his daughter's cheek."

The tenderness she exhibited made him suck in his breath as if she was touching him instead. This was his chance, his five minutes to get to know her, but the timing was off. Marlon was in his daddy mode.

Portia motioned for him to have a seat and he did. Facing him, she anchored her elbow on the back of the sofa, then rested her cheek against her arm. She chuckled softly. "Alyssa acted out the princess part, so I was the frog." She giggled, then sighed. "I thought I would grow up and marry a prince, and have two little princesses for me, and two princes for my husband." She *hmph*ed. "Some dreams never come true." She seemed to stare past him.

"I'm sorry it didn't work out with your ex. Sometimes, true love is delayed. At least I hope so." He paused when he heard Alyssa's light snore.

Portia grinned and nodded. "Looks like she's down for the count. I was really worried about my little buddy."

It was good to know she and his baby girl hit it off. What about Mikaela? He watched the emotions play across Portia's face. The woman was naturally pretty. Wonderfully made by the Master Craftsman.

"I guess it was a good thing I didn't have any children with Leonard—my ex. He was cruel to me, no telling how he would have treated our children."

"My children are the best thing that came out of my marriage. They're angels."

Portia shook her head. "It's hard when men walk away from their families, but I'll never understand how a woman can leave her babies—never."

His mother advised him not to bad mouth the girls' mother in front of them. He did his best to follow her advice. In case Alyssa was in a semiconscious state, he lowered his voice. "In hindsight, I don't think Tammy really wanted children and had them to appease me. I wanted a family, and she wanted to be free." Before he knew it, Marlon revealed Tammy's appetite for other men. "It became a game, I guess."

Portia gasped and touched his arm. "That's terrible. Sounds like Leonard's evil twin. I can't comprehend an individual taking pleasure in hurting others—mentally. He filed for divorce the day after my birthday. Then he fought me on everything we owned. Not only did he want to strip me of my dignity and things we had built together, but sanity. Sorry, I don't know why I even brought that up."

Her emotions were so raw that he was reliving the heartache with her. If Marlon wasn't holding Alyssa, he would have taken her in his arms to soothe away the pain—but that was pure fantasy. "Hey, I've been at a place before where I just wanted to process my past. I'm glad to listen. I've been there, done that," he repeated Robyn's words.

She shrugged. "It was a battle I didn't give to Christ. At one point, I seriously thought about retaliation—fire power."

"Not you," he teased, and a smile tugged at her lips. "You're too sweet for that."

"You'd be surprised what a person will do when backed in a corner."

No, I wouldn't. Marlon thought about how he lashed out in his circumstances. Since they were having a cleansing moment, he took a chance and shared. "I did retaliate." He bowed his head in shame. "What type of man lets his wife walk all over on him? I wanted a family more than anything—a perfect one—but Tammy wasn't the one. To get back at her, I stepped out of my marriage—tit-for-tat."

Portia gasped, then blinked. Disappointment reigned on her face. "You? You seem too good of a guy to stoop that low."

The atmosphere seemed to change with that one word—good.

"I did regret it and eventually repented. That wasn't the person I wanted to be. I never suspected my wife would cheat on me—or maybe I did. She was a flirt, and it just wasn't with me."

Twirling one of her ponytails, she seemed to study him. "Fornication doesn't land people in jail."

"Hell—yes. Jail—no—except for attempted murder, armed criminal action, and assault. Stepping out on me was okay—" He freed one arm from around Alyssa and patted his chest—"yet, she had a problem when I did it to her—strictly for retaliation. When she found out, she bought a gun and tried to kill me."

Portia's mouth dropped opened, but no words came out. She glanced at Alyssa again. "Well, ah, I'm glad the girls won't grow up in that environment."

"Although I can't believe how I responded to

Tammy's unfaithfulness, I still want a complete family—a wife and children."

Portia nodded. "Robyn told me how she and Derek reunited. Wow. How often does that happen?"

"That's not going to happen with my ex. She started shooting while the girls were in the house. She had no regard for their safety. Sometimes, I wonder if I hadn't cheated, would my marriage had mended. Doesn't matter. Once Tammy is released, she'll probably get back with one of her boyfriends."

Portia reached out and patted his shoulder, a gesture to provide comfort, but the touch was electric. "I hope God sends you someone special."

"Are you willing to give love a second chance?" He held his breath, waiting on an answer, waiting to see if he would have a chance to get to know her.

"Not with a cheater. I believe in being faithful."

Ouch. Was she talking about him?

When Portia stifled a yawn, Marlon couldn't believe they had been talking for almost an hour. She stood, and he took his cue that it was time to leave and possibly move on, because he had ruined his chance.

"I think she'll be fine and will sleep through the night. Let her stay. I'll sleep close to her." She reached for Alyssa.

Reluctantly, he handed her over, kissed his daughter's forehead and left.

CHAPTER FIVE

"I blew it." Marlon concluded after he returned home and collapsed in his bed. He had one chance at bat and struck out with Portia. His mother always said, "It's not the sin that overtakes you in the beginning, it's Christ's salvation that you embrace before it's your end."

"Yeah," he mumbled. Although he was steady building his commitment to Christ, it would be nice to have a partner by his side for them to grow together like Derek and Robyn. Somehow, he kept attracting the wrong kind of woman—flirtatious, drop-dead gorgeous, and eager for his company. Portia didn't appear the type, but how strong was her spiritual foundation post her divorce?

Marlon was looking for substance, heart, and pure love this time. Fool him twice, shame on him. Although he couldn't take back his actions during his marriage, with a second chance with the right woman, he would be a better man. Closing his eyes, Portia's face appeared before he drifted off.

The next morning, Marlon continued to pray for worthiness to have another relationship. If not with Portia, than a godly woman. Yet, he was thankful for all Jesus had already given him. He finished in Jesus' name, then got off his knees. Before performing his morning routine, he phoned Coy to check on Alyssa. When she answered, he heard loud high-pitched voices in the background. "How's my baby girl?"

Coy chuckled. "She's the loudest. Your daughter woke early, insisting she and Portia finish the book they were reading last night."

Marlon exhaled, then chuckled.

"See, she was fine. Just the wrong combinations of fun food last night. Sorry about alarming you again. This morning, I made plain pancakes while they watched cartoons with Portia. My sister's definitely a big kid at heart." She laughed.

Portia. Hearing her name made him regret feeling comfortable enough to be transparent. Wrong tactic. "So what time should I come to get them?"

"Give them some more play time. How about one or two this afternoon?"

"Sounds good. Thanks for letting my lovelies crash your party."

"There was no crash. They're always welcome. We had fun." He heard more laughter, then the call ended.

A few minutes after one, Marlon stood outside Coy's door and knocked. This time, the hostess opened it and invited him inside. He searched for Alyssa first. "Ally, how you feelin', my lovely?"

"Good, Daddy." Wound up, she gave him a

rundown of all the activities they had packed into their slumber party. Portia's name came up six times, because he was counting.

Marlon sensed Portia's presence before she came into his view. She looked nothing like the cartoon character she was dressed like the previous night. Her beauty brightened the room. Giving her his full attention, he spoke first. "Hi."

"Hello," she greeted him with a distance that had nothing to do with room size. She faced her sister. "Ah, Coy, the station just called. I go in this evening."

"That's good news. Get it?" Her sister grinned.

Alyssa raced to Portia, then Mikaela followed suit. They smothered her with hugs, and Marlon watched the utopia spread across her face as they whispered something and giggled. Emerald joined her friends and she giggled too. Yeah, he was possibly looking at the woman who could turn his world upside down. All he had to do was convince her that when two worlds collide, the result could be an explosion of happiness.

Portia and Coy stood in the doorway, waving goodbye to their guests. The lock barely clicked when Coy spun around with a goofy grin. "I think

Marlon likes you. I saw the way he was looking at you just now. What are you going to do about it?"

"Duh. Absolutely nothing." She turned and was about to head to the loft when Coy's comment stopped her.

"Go out with the loving father of two sweet little girls." She folded her arms as if they were in a standoff. "And thanks for asking for my advice."

"I didn't." She continued on to her makeshift bedroom to find something to wear to work. Her sister followed and perched on the sleeper.

"Hmmm, from this very spot last night, I had a bird's-eye view of you two."

Portia looked over her shoulder. "You mean after you squinted to find a sliver of an opening between the panels."

Coy shrugged. "Anyway, I caught a glimpse of a picture-perfect family. Maybe you didn't realize it, but you, Portia Marie Hunter, were in a comfort zone with him. So, in case Marlon didn't drop big enough hints, I'm telling you he likes you and you should go out with him."

Portia didn't know how she felt about Coy's perceived analysis—a psych major her sister wasn't. "Are you taking any medication that causes delusions? We chatted as we monitored Alyssa. Plus, he didn't ask me. It would be a no anyway. We swapped marriage heartache stories. I'm not repeating vulnerable behavior and getting involved with a man like my ex."

"Leonard was a jerk who only cared about himself. I never liked him, but you loved him, so I hoped I was wrong—for your sake. When your marriage ended, there was no fun in being right when you were hurting."

"I know," she said softly with a sigh.

"I get good vibes from Marlon. He's a hardworking dad." Coy stretched out on Portia's bed and crossed her arms behind her head.

"Since you're singing his praises, why don't you go out with him?"

Coy laughed. "Like my life isn't already complete with Emerald. The man never gazed at me like that. Anyway, I've been approached by many men since my divorce," she said, pausing as Portia looked at her, "but I can't. Where Leonard was a jerk, Eric was a bum."

True, her ex-brother-in-law wasn't a cheater. He only wanted the perks of being married. Before his desertion, Eric admitted he had married too soon. At thirty-five he wasn't ready to be a dad and husband. As expected, Eric didn't fight Coy about a divorce and started to pay child support, then stopped. That only infuriated her sister. Instead of going back to court, she went back to school and earned a master's in nursing to provide for herself and Emerald. She refused to beg the man for a dime. Even Eric's family made little effort to see their grandchild.

"Sis, he cheated on his wife," Portia revealed quietly.

Coy gasped, crestfallen. "And he was my hero." She started bad-mouthing the man, so Portia came to his defense.

"He says his wife cheated first and as a payback, he had an affair too." She twisted her lips. "I never heard of a worse case of tit-for-tat scenario. He says he accepted responsibility for his actions, and he should have handled his ex's betrayal better."

"Hmm. That changes things. I like him again." Coy beamed, displaying their father's lopsided signature smile.

"Hell-o." Portia waved her arms in the air, then made sure Emerald was nowhere around before she repeated. "He cheated."

"But it sounds like he regretted it." She sat up.

"Yeah, and I regret marrying Leonard, but that doesn't change the fact that I did."

"I thought you said you wanted to date and marry again."

"Yes, to the right man God sends me, and I trust Him not to send me a carbon copy of my ex. In Jesus' name. Amen."

CHAPTER SIX

"Daddy, are you going to Sunday school with us?" Mikaela asked as she began to skip alongside her father out the door.

"Not today, my lovelies. We didn't leave early enough for that." He squeezed both their hands. Going back to church had not only been a good move for him spiritually, but it made his daughters happy.

The drive to Holy Ghost Temple was a good half hour, and on the way he enjoyed his daughters' chatter about the slumber party at Ms. Coy's house and the fun things they did with Ms. Portia as if they were trying to out-best each other.

"She read to me," Alyssa said matter-of-factly.

"She showed me that bananas and blueberries make the best smoothies," Mikaela countered.

"She combed my hair and made it pretty."

"Ms. Portia combed my hair too, Ally."

Marlon looked in the rearview mirror to see Mikaela sticking out her tongue.

"Mikaela! You will not treat your sister like that," he said firmly. "Now apologize."

After puckering her lower lip, she sniffed. His daughter could summon tears in five seconds or less. "Sorry." Mikaela reached over and hugged Alyssa.

Satisfied they were back on track, Marlon smiled that Portia had left an impression on his daughters. As he neared his exit, Marlon tried to clear his head of Portia and braced himself for the onslaught of sisters that would greet him, coo over his daughters, and offer to babysit and cook dinners before suggesting a night out.

He wasn't inside the church lobby five minutes before he heard his name called. Inwardly groaning, he braced himself to be polite. He was relieved that it was Robyn who had called his name.

"Hey, brother-in-law. Saved you a seat."

"Hi, Aunt Robyn," his girls said in a singsong manner.

His sister-in-law doted on his girls with hugs and kisses before he escorted them to the children's classes. He was almost at his destination when Sister Trise Newton glided toward him with a smile and open arms.

"I don't like her, Daddy," Mikaela said immediately.

"Mikaela, that's not nice. Keep your voice down."

"But Daddy," she said, pouting, "I don't think she likes kids like Ms. Portia, because she's always yellin—"

"That's enough, sweetheart." He rubbed her back. She was in a sentimental mood this morning. "Good morning." He mustered a smile.

She leaned in to greet him with air kisses on both his cheeks, but he discreetly stepped back. "My offer still stands for a home-cooked meal."

"He gets plenty at my house, Sister Newton," his mother said sweetly, appearing at their side and rescuing him.

"Grandma!" Mikaela and Alyssa screamed their delight and hugged his mother.

"Thanks." Marlon nodded at Sister Newton, then kissed his mom. Taking his girls' hands, he excused himself and proceeded to their classrooms, then hastily made his way to the sanctuary and sat with his family.

Once the praise segment had concluded, the choir sang their rendition of "You Have Won the Victory." Afterward Pastor Kinder stepped to the podium and greeted visitors, made a few announcements, then opened his Bible. "Victory— yes victory."

He paused. "Sometimes, saints forget we're on the winning side. The choice was already made for you. It's up to you whether you want to stay on Jesus' team. Consider which is the best choice. What has the devil promised you? God has promised you redemption, forgiveness, eternal life, and the list goes on. What are you struggling with today?"

Every sin that a man doeth is without the body; but he that commits fornication sins against his own body. Yep, 1 Corinthians 6:18 summed it up. Forgiveness, Marlon didn't answer aloud. Yes, He knew God had forgiven him, but when would he forgive himself for such a grievous act?

"I know your struggle is real," Pastor Kinder said, invading his thoughts. "The Bible says in 1 Peter 5:7: *Casting all your care upon him; for he cares for you.'* That alone should lighten your load. Lord, I need a job—check. Lord—I need to make my house mortgage… Lord, I desire a mate. Listen, your impossible is possible with God. Thank Him, ask Him, but don't forget to add if it be Your will..."

Marlon was listening. Nothing Pastor Kinder said he hadn't heard before, but his heart was pricked. What was God's will for him and his daughters?

I will reveal it to you in due season, God whispered.

That week, Marlon found himself building his faith with meditating on the Scriptures, even while Portia faded in and out of his mind. *Lord, I know I'm not worthy of her affections, but I'm drawn to her, even my girls are. Please either open her eyes to see my heart,* he paused, not wanting to concede defeat, but Jesus knew what he was about to say anyway, *or to send the right one for me.*

At first, he didn't think much about not seeing Portia during his twice weekly pickups at school, thinking she was working, then curiosity got the best of him. He asked Coy.

"Oh, she's at home battling the flu, so I'm on nurse duty at work and home."

"Does she need anything? Is there something I can do?" He asked, concerned.

Coy had a strange expression as a slow grin stretched across her face. "If you can check on her later, that would be great. I'll be at work and I'm taking Emerald to the onsite daycare with me, so she won't get sick."

"Done." Instead of going straight home, he made a detour. "Mom, I need a favor."

"What is it, son?" she asked, surprised at his appearance, considering he'd picked up the girls.

"Can you make a pot of homemade soup?"

"Who's sick? Are my babies..." She craned her neck to have a look at her granddaughters.

"No," he said sheepishly, then lowered his voice. "For Portia, Coy's sister."

"Hmm. Isn't that nice?" Lane didn't hide her amusement. "A woman appreciates when a man does sweet things for her." He lifted a brow. "Really? Mom, you act as if I've never been married before."

Hmph. "It's been a while. I guess you'd better wash your hands and get to dicing up carrots, celery..."

"You're making me cook?" He couldn't believe it.

"She's your girlfriend," she teased and broke into a fit of giggles.

Within an hour, Marlon had completed his task with pride while his mother busied herself with baking cornbread. She sliced off a healthy serving for Portia and Coy. "You might want to stop by the store for orange juice. This is really a sweet gesture, son. Before your dad and I divorced, I started to believe he didn't care." She became quiet and seemed sad. She perked up, then continued. "This shows you care. Not only is she a pretty girl and sweet, but Robyn says she's been wounded. This may help her heal."

Marlon nodded. He knew all about healing. "I'm going to run an errand. Stay with Grandma, and I'll be back soon, okay?" he advised his daughters.

"Where you going, Daddy?" Mikaela asked.

"To visit a sick friend," he explained.

"Can Ally and I go too?" She looked hopeful. If his daughter knew he was heading over to Emerald's house, she might demand to drive.

"No, I don't want you to get sick." He kissed each of them on the forehead and turned to leave.

"Is it Ms. Portia? She's nice and fun" Mikaela pressed him. She looked concerned.

His mother snickered under her breath from her spot nearby.

"And how do you know that?" he asked, squinting.

"I heard you ask Ms. Coy about her."

His daughter was too smart for her own good. "You still can't go."

"But what if you get sick?"

"Then you can be my nurse."

"Yay, we get to be Daddy's nurses," Mikaela said, jumping up and down as if that was a good thing. Alyssa mimicked her older sister. "We're going to pray right now for her. C'mon on, Ally." They disappeared into the other room.

Marlon left and made the stop for juice. On his way to the checkout, he spied the greeting cards section. He read a few and chose one where the words seemed heartfelt. He grabbed it and headed to the register.

He got to Coy's house in no time. Marlon rang the doorbell. After a few seconds, he knocked. He was about to ring again when it opened slowly and Portia squinted.

"Marlon? What are you doing here?" She coughed, and it seemed to take the wind out of her. "It's a bad time. I'm sick."

"I know. That's why I'm here." He lifted the bags. "May I come in? I made you soup." He held his breath, not because he was afraid of catching germs—he'd had his flu shot—but he hoped she wouldn't turn him away.

Most days, she was beautiful. Today wasn't one of those days. Yet, even in her weakened state, there was no denying her underlying loveliness.

She sniffed. "What little I can smell, it smells good."

He grinned. "Yep." She stepped back, and he entered, towering over her for the briefest moment. He hadn't been this close to her since the night of the pajama party.

Portia shuffled her way toward the kitchen, and he trailed her. Setting things on the table, he took the liberty of searching the cabinets for a bowl as she flopped in a chair. She appeared exhausted by the task.

Marlon didn't waste time as he filled the bowl, carved off a chunk of cornbread and poured orange juice into a glass, then slid everything in front of her.

"Thanks," she whispered, then asked God to bless her food. Portia took a few sips and pushed it away, barely holding up her head.

"What's wrong? I made it myself. You don't like it?" Marlon's heart dropped in disappointment.

"Too tired to eat." She covered her face. "Thank

you, but I need to lay down," she mumbled through her hands.

"You also need your strength." He scooted over, and his parental instincts kicked in. Taking the spoon, Marlon scooped up the soup and began to force feed her.

"You might get sick," she fussed between slurps.

I hope not. "Nah. I got my flu shot."

"I should've gotten one too. Some of my coworkers have it...I missed out on hours that I could've worked. This won't happen...next year." Her strength seemed to be returning. He watched as she sampled the orange juice, then declined more.

"Okay. I'll let that slide." He winked.

She mustered a smile in return.

"How do you feel?"

"A little better."

Standing, he gathered the dirty dishes to wash, then thought about the card. Marlon retrieved the envelope from the bag and handed it to her.

"Until your strength returns, rest and know I'm praying for you to get better. May Jesus breathe healing into your body. Amen," she whispered, "Signed Marlon and the girls."

Portia glanced up at him with misty eyes, either from the illness or she was touched. "Awww. That's so sweet... I don't know the last time I got a card."

She had a faraway look in her eyes. "Or even been sick." She reached for her orange juice and took small sips.

Her appetite was bouncing back when she asked for another piece of the cornbread.

Marlon grinned. "Coming right up." He cut another slice, then wrapped the remainder for later. "I guess I'd better let you get some more rest."

"I've been laying in the bed for days. Maybe I'll clean up." She tried to stand.

Marlon gently rested his hand on her shoulder. "I don't think that's a good idea. You need to rest."

"That's all I've been doing is resting. Want to watch a movie with me?" Her hopeful smile reminded him of Mikaela and Alyssa.

He chuckled. "Okay. Maybe for a little while. Only to keep an eye on you, so that you rest."

"Thank you. Get the remote, find a movie and I'll freshen up…as best as a patient can."

"I really want you to rest," he said, still concerned, even though she looked better.

"You're sweet." Although moving slowly, Portia seemed to have more energy as she climbed the stairs to the loft.

Sooner than he expected, she returned, wearing a fresh T-shirt. Face washed and her messy hair was brushed into a ponytail. "Find something?"

He enjoyed her playful nature. *Lord, open the*

door to her heart. "There's a Hallmark movie." He hoped it was filled with romance.

Mikaela grinned as she knelt at her bedside to say her prayers. Her daddy liked Ms. Portia, but he didn't come back sick, so she and Alyssa wouldn't have any fun playing his nurse. She pouted. Maybe next time. Closing her eyes, she whispered, "Jesus, it's almost Christmas…" She opened her eyes. She needed help. Her Sunday school teacher quoted from the Bible that two are better than one, and where two or more are gathered together, Jesus was there too.

Getting up, she looked at her sister in the other bed, then shook her. "Ally, wake up," she whispered. "We've got to pray together for another mommy."

When she barely stirred, Mikaela carefully dragged Alyssa out the bed. A heavy sleeper, Alyssa didn't open an eye. Instead her sister was fast asleep with her head resting on the mattress although she was kneeling.

Mikaela scooted next to Alyssa, draped her arm around her sister's shoulder. "Jesus, Alyssa is praying too in her sleep, so can we get a new mommy by Christmas?"

CHAPTER SEVEN

It was the middle of the night and Portia couldn't believe she was in the kitchen for another serving of Marlon's homemade soup. Not only was it tasty, but she felt her strength returning.

The man had risked his life—people died from severe cases of the flu per Nurse Coy—to see about her. Marlon had been a godsend. Although her fever had broken earlier that morning, she was still weak and surprised she'd gotten up to answer the door. Portia had grown accustomed to being alone in sickness and in health during the latter part of her marriage, so the gesture touched her.

One day Leonard loved her, then the next, he despised her. She didn't know what turned him against her until the day of their divorce. He was living two lives—married with a chick on the side. Well, the chick won a defective prize.

Marlon had been patient, tender, and focused on spoon-feeding her. How humbling to have a man see her at her worse and not be repulsed.

"You'll never guess who stopped by," Portia said when Coy called to check on her not long after Marlon left. "Marlon," Portia didn't give her a chance to answer. She smiled.

It was as if her sister could see Portia's face. "Interesting. How can you deny a brother who visits the sick a chance?" Coy teased. "He did ask about you earlier when I picked up Emerald."

"Did he tell you he was going to make me soup?"

"Nope. Wow, he's a keeper. It's a shame we married the bad guys, and some other women walk away from the good ones." A page blared in the background. "Listen, I've got to go, but you should think three times before walking away from possibilities."

Portia blinked, not realizing her thoughts had drifted while she scooped up the broth until the spoon scrapped the bottom of the bowl. Getting up, she steadied herself, still a little dizzy. She walked to the sink, rinsed the bowl, and made her way back to the loft.

Once she slid back under the covers, Marlon's handsome face appeared and so did Leonard's, even in her dreams, the man knew how to ruin a good moment. Both were handsome, but Marlon had more rawness to his looks where, if Portia admitted it, Leonard was a pretty boy, but peering into his soul, cruelty and loveless were vivid. Marlon's eyes were warm and captive, and she saw a glimpse of his wounded spirit that had once consumed her too, but there was something else she saw—his regret...and possibilities.

Could she trust a man again, especially one who

retaliated with a tit-for-tat deed? Would Marlon hurt her? Could she survive a second blow? Although Leonard cheated on her, cheating never entered her mind.

You cheated Me out of My praise when you walked away from Me, God admonished her.

She sighed. This was taking too much brain power when she should be resting. If Marlon wanted to bring honesty to the table, Portia would see how deep he would go. Then she would have to be honest with herself. She had to repent for not forgiving Leonard sincerely, so she could move on.

With loving kindness, I have drawn you. Marlon is showing you his loving kindness, God whispered into her ear as she drifted to sleep.

By mid-October, Marlon started to take overtime to tuck away money for Christmas to give his girls whatever they had on their lists. His mother said he was spoiling them. Marlon argued it was his right as their dad.

It was almost seven in the evening when he dragged his tired body into his mother's house to eat whatever she cooked and take his girls home. He would have enough time to hear all about their day, go over their homework, and read them a story before bed.

They screamed their delight at his presence and lavished him with hugs and kisses. Mikaela took off for her backpack, pulled out an envelope, then hurried back to him.

"It's a card from Ms. Portia." She beamed. "I get cards from my friends for Valentine's Day. Do you think it's a Valentine's card?"

Marlon smirked. He loved the innocence of his daughters. "I don't know." He lifted each girl in his arms and walked toward the kitchen.

"Open it and see, Daddy," Mikaela insisted.

"Not now." Marlon's heart pounded, wanting to do just that. "Later."

"Hey, son." His mother chuckled. "She's been waiting to give that to you since I picked her up." She eyed the clock. "You're later than usual."

"I know." Setting the girls down, he glanced around the kitchen at the pots on the stove. He preceded to the sink to wash his hands. "And I'm beat." Uncovering the lids, Marlon began to help himself.

Stuffed and patting his stomach, Marlon kissed his mother goodbye and drove home. Once he took care of his daddy duties, he retired to the privacy of his bedroom. Mikaela had asked twice if he had opened Ms. Portia's card. He didn't know who was more eager, his daughter or himself.

He rubbed his hand over the envelope. This was the first time since meeting Portia that she had reached out to him. He surmised it was a thank-you note. Should he be hopeful that it contained more?

Tearing the seal, Marlon slowly slipped out the card. Was that a scent of her perfume he whiffed? He had seen greeting cards before and knew there were African-American lines like Mahogany and Our Voices. This was from neither. The artist was masterful in the sketching a black woman whose lips curled up in a blissful expression. The woman didn't resemble Portia, but he imagined it was her smile just the same.

He stared at it until he had the courage to open it. *When I was sick, you visited me. When I was weak, you prayed for me. Thank you for showing me how much you cared. Your recovered patient, Portia Hunter.* She scribbled her own smiley face. He chuckled.

Do you think we can have dinner again when I'm not sick? Ground rules: I'm not spoon feeding you.

Marlon barked out a laugh, then quieted, hoping he didn't wake his girls. "Lord, thank You for the flu. In Jesus' name. Amen," he mumbled, then silently repented just as fast. Portia had been very ill, and he wouldn't want to see her or anyone battle that virus. He reached for his phone.

He called the number Portia listed. When her strong and sultry voice answered, Marlon had to recapture his breath. "Thank you for the card. You've made my day." He grinned.

"I'm glad," she said softly.

"Let me treat you to dinner. Name the place and day."

"Hmm. Sounds like a date," Portia said, making Marlon wonder if she was teasing him.

"Is that a bad thing?"

"Before Nurse Washington made a house call, I wouldn't consider it. Now…"

"Portia, you've got to talk to me," he coaxed, hoping she would open up to him again.

"Well, I really enjoyed your company and would like to know more about you, but…" She sighed.

"But?"

"I'm scared. *Whew*." She seemed relieved she'd gotten it out.

"If God is our focus, He can help us together to be overcomers. How about a mid-week movie?" he blurted out, forgetting he had planned to work overtime the next couple of days.

"I hadn't expected so soon."

"I wasn't expecting you to walk into my life."

"Hmmm, so the answer is yes. See you tomorrow."

CHAPTER EIGHT

"Finally." Coy leaned on the doorway of the hall bathroom.

"Oh, stop it. I know my hair was long overdue," Portia defended while towel-drying her freshly shampooed hair. Salon visits, including manicures, still weren't an option as long as she had a car note, attorney fees, and an unsteady job that hadn't called all week.

"Yeah that too, but I was talking about going out with Marlon." Coy broke out in a happy dance. "See, St. Louis does have better attractions than Kansas City, and I'm not talking about amusement parks."

"True." Portia squeezed a creamy conditioner in her hands, then began to massage it into her hair. There was something about the man that intrigued her. Maybe it was his vulnerability intertwined with his strength.

Turning around, she stared at her big sister and sighed. "I wouldn't start celebrating yet. This is a big step for me." She wiped away a trail of water running down her face. "I've been second-guessing myself all day. I'm almost scared that I will really like him, then what? Any other woman who had to deal with Leonard's shenanigans probably wouldn't marry again for life."

Coy put her hands on Portia's shoulders. "Forget

him. Any other woman would probably have beaten him down with one stiletto, then went after the hussy with the other one. That's the way I felt with Eric, not because of any infidelity, but because of his abandonment, but he wasn't worth me breaking a heel anyway."

"Umm-mmm." Her sister protested too much, feigning to be a man-eater, but sadness from her failed marriage lingered in her eyes, even after six years.

"I admire my little sister who despite the horror still believes in love...and I do too—from afar. Very, very far away."

"Yeah, barely. That's my revenge, to be happy. I wish you—"

Coy held up her hand to stop her. "Nope. Don't go there. Eric and I knew each other since grade school. That's what hurt to the core—we knew each other—we were good friends, neighbors, like family—or at least I thought I knew him." She sighed. "Clearly, I missed the red flags, so shame on me. Anyway, I've got the most precious gift— Emerald. You don't have anyone. I want to see you with a husband, and I think Marlon is an exceptional father."

Suddenly, Portia's phone rang, and she took off for the loft, hiking two stairs at a time. Eying the station's number flashed on the screen, she grinned.

Work! Looking over her shoulder, she gave Coy the thumbs-up, then answered.

"Hey, Portia. Candy called from the ER," her boss began, "she broke her leg. Can you work her shift this evening and next week until I can rearrange the schedule?"

"Absolutely. I'll be there by two." She ended the call with renewed hope. She went in search of the blow dryer. Ponytail coming up as she gave Coy a recap.

"I'm glad you're getting more hours."

"Me too. Praise God. I need the money."

"And you need a Prince Charming. I hope you won't use work as an excuse to make Marlon work overtime for your affections. And since we're on the subject of pay—"

"Ah, we're not."

"Don't make Marlon pay for what another man did," Coy continued as if Portia hadn't said a word.

A week later, Portia craved rest. After clocking in fifty-three hours at the station, she was drained. The good news, she had four days off. She had just rolled over and hugged her pillow tighter when Emerald's high-pitched voice echoed throughout the condo.

The girl's chatter grew louder, stopping at

Portia's bed. "Auntie, Miss Robyn invited Mommy, and me and you to her Hallelujah Party."

Robyn. She had meant to call her for lunch, but it had been a crazy news week. Oh well, maybe next time. With her face smashed against the pillow, Portia mumbled, "A Hallelujah what?"

"It's a party, and you have to come."

"Can't. Sleepy." Portia heard herself snore, then everything faded to black again, even though her eyes were already closed.

Too soon, her sister nudged her. "Why don't you come with us? We've both missed church lately, so this can be our dose of inspiration."

"I've been reading my Bible throughout the day. I'll take a party rain check."

"Come on. They say it's their Christian alternative to Halloween, and I'm curious." Coy shoved her over, causing Portia to squint. She blinked until her sister and niece's faces came into focus. "I'm sure Marlon will be there." Coy grinned.

His name gave her pause. Portia did feel bad about canceling a date that *she* had suggested. With trying to secure a full-time position, she didn't have the luxury of saying, no. Marlon said he understood. Plus, they had communicated a few times through texts, "Have a good day", "What's your thoughts on this Scripture?" or "I miss seeing you."

"Girl, do you see the way I look, besides I don't

have a costume." She eyed her sister and Emerald's getups.

"Trust me, you looked worse when you were sick, so you're wearing your costume." Coy laughed. "Seriously. Nothing elaborate. We're Biblical characters, and I've got the perfect character for you." She threw back the covers. "Get up, shower, and add mouthwash after brushing your teeth, then I'll transform you."

"Please. You should see yourself after a twelve-hour shift." Against her better judgment, Portia conceded. Six hours wasn't enough rest for her beauty and brain cells. She didn't scrimp on her bath, but when she stepped out of the tub, the mad rush was on as she had to hurry to apply her makeup.

"You're going to be Queen Esther." Coy began to finger comb Portia's hair up on top of her head and used one of Emerald's tiaras to contain it. Her niece giggled and left them alone.

"Remember when we were little and Halloween was second to Christmas?" Portia mused, watching Coy.

Her sister nodded. "And our birthdays."

Hmph. "Right now, my birthdays have been a source of pain, served with divorced papers, then the dissolution granted two years later, ironically the day after my birthday."

"I know," Coy said quietly, "but you're here

now and creating good memories."

From her hair to makeup to a long sleek formal her sister had worn to a company Christmas party many years ago, that her sister claimed she could no longer wear, Portia blinked at her reflection. Portia had forgotten she still had curves.

Twenty minutes later, the trio was out the door and on the way to the party. Portia admired the landscapes. Kirkwood had many affluent areas. It was the norm for one neighborhood to upstage another with larger homes and professional manicured lawns. When Coy turned on Robyn's street, Portia's mouth dropped. To prove her point, Robyn and Derek's house was a magnificent story and a half. It would put the house she and Leonard had built in Kansas City to shame. "Ooh."

"I know. With all these personal property taxes, you see why this school district has the bucks." Once Coy parked, they got out, each taking one of Emerald's hands.

Portia's phone alerted her to a text at the same time as they were about to enter Robyn's house.

She scanned the message as she crossed the threshold. `My brother is having a party. If you're not too tired, please come.`

Portia smiled when he appeared at her side. He looked pleased to see her. "Here."

He chuckled, and his eyes twinkled as he squeezed her hand. "Yes, you are, and you're beautiful."

The slight gesture seemed to set off powerful shockwaves around her. Blushing, she looked away and noticed Derek, Robyn and other adults were sporting black T-shirts with colorful images of superheroes. Jesus was in the middle of them. A quote underneath read, "That's how I saved the world." It was a profound message that she had seen promoted on social media.

She swallowed to break the trance. He wore the same T-shirt, and it showcased his every muscle, which her sister could probably name.

Staring back into his eyes was a mistake. He was pulling her in as he smirked.

"I'm guessing your Biblical character is either Queen Esther or Queen Candace. Both were beautiful and as exotic as you are. Your ex was a fool."

Portia blushed. "Thank you for saying what I concluded too."

"I think every queen needs an escort." He held out his arm, and she rested her hand on his forearm and allowed him to lead her through the maze of guests until she reached Robyn.

As the two women began to chat, Marlon pulled her away. "Just so you know, we're nine days overdue on our date, and I plan to collect within twenty-four hours."

The seriousness in Marlon's rich brown eyes dared her to call his bluff.

Marlon didn't care that it wasn't a date. He wasn't about to let Portia out of his sight. "Robyn made a nice spread. Would you like for me to fix you a plate?"

"Yes, please."

"I'll be right back." At the table, he grabbed a plate and began to scoop pasta on it.

Mikaela popped up at his side. "Is that for Ms. Portia?"

He gave his daughter a side-eye. Nothing seemed to slip past her. "Yes."

"Can I help?" Without waiting for permission, she became the maestro and pointed to different dishes, but was adamant about the fruit salad. "Emerald says her aunt likes apples and bananas, because she eats them every morning."

Good to know. He nodded.

As Marlon left the table, Mikaela had grabbed a wad of napkins, along with utensils, and marched beside him.

Portia glanced up and her exotic eyes sparkled. God, how could this beautiful creature have been mistreated? The question continued to nag him.

You mistreated your wife, the devil taunted and Marlon's high spirits plummeted.

He was washed in My blood and restored. I forgave him! God called checkmate.

With that boost, he smiled. "Madam." He handed her the plate and a cup of punch. "My sidekick." He tilted his head toward Mikaela.

"I'm not your sidekick, Daddy. I'm your daughter." Mikaela presented her utensils and gave Portia a hug.

"Thank you, beautiful daughter and father."

"My daddy's handsome, not pretty," Mikaela said matter-of-factly, then ran off to play with some of her friends.

"I stand corrected." Portia blushed, bowed her head and silently gave thanks. Marlon watched her every movement. He couldn't help it. He missed seeing her, and had no good excuse to show up on her job just to get a glimpse to satisfy his hunger. She was beautiful and wounded.

He knew it took time for him to heal after his divorce. He wanted to shower Portia with support, comfort, whatever she needed to be made whole again.

Pray for her, God whispered, referencing Romans 12:15-16: *Rejoice with them that do rejoice, and weep with them that weep. Be of the same mind one toward another. Mind not high things, but condescend to men of low estate. Be not wise in your own conceits.*

Marlon did as instructed. With Portia in his presence, he barely noticed the children swarming around them in Biblical costumes. This was the second year his brother and sister-in-law hosted such a party since they'd remarried. They always found a reason to celebrate love—theirs, their children, or God's. And, they went all out. This year, the costumes were more elaborate.

When Portia finished, she faced him with a smile. "I thought it was too much food. I didn't realize I was that hungry. And the fruit—fresh." She closed her eyes in appreciation.

Kudos to Mikaela. He grinned. "My sidekick picked the fruit."

"Brownie point for her. She is sooo sweet."

"What about me?" He tilted his head, fishing for any compliment she would give him.

She laughed but didn't answer as a few of the children took center stage talking about Biblical heroes or other characters.

He couldn't remember the boy's name, but Marlon knew he was in the same class with his nephew Tyler.

"I'm Moses," he said with a long white beard that hung passed his waist. He had fake white brushy brows too. "From a baby, God protected me. God loved me, and I got a chance to do miracles! Not magic, but big—" the boy spread his arms in the air—"big miracles like parting the Red Sea and siccing bugs on mean Pharaoh."

The audience chuckled at his dialogue, then clapped before the child worked the room with his big bag for the guests to place treats.

"Oh, I didn't know I was to bring anything," Portia whispered. Her brows knit together with concern.

"It's optional. My sister-in-law provides bowls of treats for the adults to give to the children after they finish."

"Oh." She bobbed her head.

When Emerald took center stage, Portia stood and hurried into the dining room. She returned with fists full of candy and fruit treats. She seemed smug as she wiggled next to him. "Got it."

"I see." Liking her carefree spirit, he laughed at her playfulness.

"My name is Zipporah." Emerald lifted her chin. "I was Moses' second wife. I was a beautiful Ethiopian woman and God didn't let people talk bad about me, not even Moses' sister." She rambled off a few facts, then took a bow. Portia was on her feet cheering while Coy clapped the loudest. When her niece made her way around the room for treats, Portia gave her a hug and was generous with her goodies.

"This is fun," she said almost breathless, beaming at Marlon, then nudged him.

The brush against Marlon's arms tickled the hairs on his arm under his shirt. The woman knew how to heighten his senses without trying.

After a couple more performances, it was Marlon's nephew Tyler's turn. Marlon's brother Derek had his phone ready to record his son who was wearing a gold helmet.

"I'm a centurion. I'm strong and mighty and command warriors. I'm special because Jesus healed my daughter because of my faith."

Of all the children, his nephew was the most animated, indicating Derek or Robyn—possibly both—had coached him as if it was a major production.

"I had faith that God was going to put my mommy and daddy back together again," Tyler stated.

"I doubt that was part of his script," Marlon whispered to Portia who was patting her chest. It appeared to be an emotional moment as *ahh*s floated around them, and Derek grabbed Robyn around the waist and tugged her to his side.

Tyler received the most standing ovation.

Shaking her head, Portia sniffed. "I guess it's a good thing I never had children with my ex."

"But you said you wanted two girls and two boys?" Marlon grew concerned. His daughters were a package deal. Say the word, and he would back off.

"And you remembered that? I still do, and that's the sad part."

Marlon exhaled so hard that he felt lightheaded, but was relieved.

Soon, Mikaela and Alyssa made their appearance. His mother had sewn colorful long robes that fit their tiny bodies. There was nothing fancy about them, but the glow on his daughters' faces made them regal. Marlon whistled, and to his surprise, Portia tried to mimic him. She failed.

"They're so cute," she complimented instead. "You and my sister are great single parents."

Marlon choked. "That's my Brownie point. Thank you."

"I'm Mary Magdalene," Mikaela declared, hushing him. Giving his full attention, Marlon puffed out his chest in pride. His daughter didn't have a shy bone in her body. "And my sister is Mary too." Alyssa nodded and smiled. She took a bow before it was time and the adults chuckled. "We both were at the tomb of Jesus. It was empty because He's

Alive!"

"Amens," floated around the room.

Lord, thank You for my little lovelies.

As the Hallelujah party wound down, guests, with wrapped carryout plates, thanked Robyn and Derek for the invite and a good time.

Finally, Marlon was about to steal some private moments with Portia, but Robyn appeared and foiled his plan.

"Halloween in a few days has nothing on our Hallelujahs." His sister-in-law lifted her hand, and Portia gave Robyn a high five while Marlon tried to give her a hint to beat it.

Either Robyn didn't see his signals, or ignored them, so he spelled it out for her. "Sorry, sis. Talk to Portia on your own time." Grabbing Portia's hand—which was incredibly soft, he regulated his breathing as he pulled her away as Robyn smarted off.

"Did you forget this is my house—"

"Our house, babe," Derek said, coming to Marlon's rescue.

Marlon nodded his thanks. Leading Portia to the nook off the kitchen, he allowed her to sit, then relaxed next to her, he stretched out his legs. He would not be rushed. Their absence had somehow magnified his affection toward her. He yearned to wrap her in his arms, or brush his lips against hers. He missed the simple pleasures of being in a relationship: holding hands, stealing kisses, and the flirting. "Now, about that date. Tomorrow evening?"

Her shoulders slumped as she pouted. "Coy has to work, so I'll have Emerald, and I promised her we would play games once we finished her homework." He hid his smile that she seemed as disappointed as he was.

"I'll babysit," his mother and Robyn said in unison, peeping their heads in the doorway.

"Does this house have any privacy?" Marlon couldn't get rid of them. At least his sister-in-law was now on his side.

"No," the women said in a sing-song tone.

"O-okay." Portia blushed.

"Since tomorrow's Sunday, why not make a day of it? Start at church while the day is young," his mother suggested.

Portia's lips curled upward as she seemed to give it some thought, then she nodded. "I like that." She turned to him for confirmation.

"Me too." He exhaled. If they kept God in the forefront, they could mend and grow together, not just the physical attraction, but nurture each other's soul with the Word. While they were making plans, Coy announced it was time to go. He left not long after Portia.

"Daddy," Mikaela said as she strapped herself into her seat. "If you marry Ms. Portia, then Emerald and I will be sisters."

Sisters. Marlon withheld his amusement. He would have to go over the family tree with his daughter. "Why do you think I should marry her?"

"Because God answers prayers," she said matter-of-factly as he started the car and drove away.

Yes, He does, Marlon mused to himself.

CHAPTER NINE

Saturday night, Portia read Marlon's text. Can't wait to see you tomorrow.

Lowering her guards, she was excited, nervous, scared....and hopeful. The last part surprised her, because she wanted to downplay her emotions around Marlon until she knew he could be trusted with her heart. I'm looking forward to it.

I think we should have a favorite Scripture. Think about it. Sleep well. Pick you and Emerald up for church in the a.m.

She scanned through the hall closets that held some of her clothes. A green dress that still bore the price tag caught her attention. It was evidence of the past when she splurged with no cares about bills. Would Marlon like her in this? she wondered for the first time in forever that she cared about what a man thought.

She smiled, recalling his suggestion that they share their favorite Scripture. Marlon was going to make her think long and hard. As she frowned, Jeremiah 29:11 came to mind, then she thought about the sparrow in Matthew 6:26. Through her heartache, Portia had never gone hungry or worried about where she would sleep. He had blessed her going out and coming back home. God had provided for her comfort when she couldn't comfort herself. Yes, this would be her favorite scripture: *Behold the fowls of the air: for they sow not, neither do they reap, nor gather into barns; yet your heavenly Father feeds them. Are ye not much better than they?*

On her knees, she prayed, "Lord, I'm surrendering my life, my relationship—if we decide on one—and my cares to You." She continued to thank and petition God until her burdens were lifted. After saying, "In Jesus' name. Amen," Portia slid under the covers, then stared at the ceiling. Whenever in doubt, Missourians always quoted the state motto "Show-me State." Marlon was starting to show her that he was completely different from Leonard. "Amen again."

The next morning, she woke refreshed. Emerald was excited that she would get to spend another day with her best friends.

Green was also her niece's favorite color, because she had beautiful eyes, courtesy of her father. Any shade of green would enhance them.

"Auntie, we can be twins today," Emerald said between slurps of her favorite cereal.

Portia chuckled. "Yes, we can, sweetie." She tweaked her cheek, remembering when her mother would dress her and Coy alike.

At nine-thirty, the bell rang. Portia opened the door, and her knees weakened. Marlon a deep green corduroy suit jacket with black slacks--nice. They both stood speechless until Emerald severed the trance. "Mr. Washington has flowers!"

That's when she blinked and glanced at his hand.

"I do. Nice color." He winked, then added, "One for each of you ladies."

Emerald accepted and was about to race to the car where his daughters were waving, but Portia stopped her. "Put on your coat, young lady."

"Allow me." Marlon's deep voice make her shiver. Once he performed the task, he gave her the same treatment.

Cherished. That's how she felt. Let chivalry live forever! "Thank you." After locking the door, Portia removed Emerald's booster seat from her car, which Marlon secured in his in no time. All three girls in the back were twirling their roses, and vying for her attention, which she didn't disappoint. She gave them hugs, and received their kisses before settling in the front seat, then sniffing her flower's fragrance.

"Ready to begin our—"

"Ready," the trio shouted from the backseat.

Exchanging amused glances with Marlon, Portia chuckled. This was what a family felt like—mom, dad, and children—nice.

For the next half hour, they chatted about their families, likes, dislikes, and their favorite Scriptures and why.

Surprisingly, when Marlon quoted, Romans 5:8: *But God commends his love toward us, in that, while we were yet sinners, Christ died for us'."* He shook his head. "That Scripture was my sword to fight off the devil's taunting. I didn't deserve to be forgiven—" he lowered his voice—"for the mistakes in my marriage, but God forgave me. I'm forever grateful."

His vulnerability was attractive. She had to forgive her ex, really forgive him, so she could grow spiritually. Portia had already repented for not consulting God about whether Leonard was His choice for a mate. She wouldn't make that mistake again.

Marlon couldn't explain it, but it felt different walking into Holy Ghost Temple's sanctuary with the girls and Portia. Instead of attending the children's classes, the girls begged to remain in the "big" church with them. He consented after consulting with Portia.

The sisters who would have made a beeline toward them, stood on the sideline, eying their competition without Portia having a clue. There was no contest. Portia Hunter was in a class all by herself.

He waved at his family who usually saved a seat

for him. Since there were five of them today, Marlon staked claim to the pew behind the Washingtons. Derek, Robyn and his mother greeted Portia warmly.

The atmosphere was charged with energy after the praise team led the congregation through a variety of worship songs.

Pastor Kinder approached the podium. "Whew. Did we just get a spiritual workout in the presence of the Lord, or what?" He scanned the sanctuary, nodding. "That same workout needs to be our routine regimen, if we're to fight the wickedness that seems to reign in our world today. It's predicted, but God promises His strength to be overcomers. In a few days, people across the country will celebrate Halloween, the spirit of witchcraft. Let this celebration be not named among the saints."

The chorus of "Amens" were loud throughout the sanctuary. His family was no exception, especially since they honored God before the devil had his reign for a night.

Pastor Kinder directed them to Ephesians six. "God talks about spiritual armor to fight. Our enemies today aren't a particular country, but a mindset. Verse twelve lets us know what we're up against. *'For we wrestle not against flesh and blood, but against principalities, against powers, against the rulers of the darkness of this world, against spiritual wickedness in high places.'* These are the last days, and the love of many are waxed cold, so don't be surprised by the abundance of wickedness, be vigilant..."

Marlon wasn't expecting to hear this message, but as his mother reminded him from time to time, "God tells us what He wants us to know. Pay attention!"

Portia seemed as riveted throughout the sermon until the pastor closed his Bible and asked everyone to stand for the altar call. Numerous people hurried toward the front for prayers from waiting ministers. He had been in that prayer line several times after the demise of his marriage until he surrendered his burdens, confessed his sins, and consented to the baptism in Jesus name and God filled his mouth with His heavenly language. To his surprise, armed with spiritual strengths didn't stop the devil from taunting him.

As he witnessed dozens to be buried in water in Jesus' name for their sins to be washed away, his heart pounded as a couple of them emerged , speaking in a heavenly language the Holy Ghost was orchestrating as evidence of His presence.

I can keep you from falling, and present you faultless before Me, God whispered and directed him to Jude 1. *This time, you have to want to be kept!*

Marlon's eyes misted. Forgetting about those around him, he bowed his head and closed his eyes.

He found himself in a secret place with God where he quietly communed with and worshipped Jesus.

He hadn't realized he had zoned out until his daughters' chatter pulled him back to the present. Opening his eyes, he noted the benediction had been given. He stood, then watched as Portia gave them some small tokens. Whatever it was, it earned her hugs from Mikaela and Alyssa.

"Look, Daddy," Mikaela showed him a stress ball from Portia that bared the television station's logo.

"I hope you don't mind, stations always have an over-stock of promotional stuff to give away. I grabbed one for Emerald and thought about your girls. I waited until after service to give it to them."

He was touched. "Thanks for thinking of them."

"Of course." She patted her heart. "They're in here."

Despite the buzz of activity around them, they were locked in a stare. Were they both stalling?

"I guess you two better get going. It's only twenty-four hours in a day, and twelve of them are already gone," his mother said with teasing in her eyes.

"Ready?" Marlon asked. When she nodded, he leaned down and kissed each daughter, then hugged them. "Be good for Grandma," he instructed. Standing again, he smiled at Portia and assisted her with her coat, but his girls didn't budge until Portia gave them hugs goodbye like she had given Emerald. The slightest contact sent shivers down his arm. He exhaled.

Without the children as chaperones, they crossed the parking lot in an uncomfortable silence between them. When Portia chuckled, he turned and asked, "What's funny?"

She shrugged, then giggled. "I'm going on a date," she said in awe.

"Yes, we are, and I'm honored that you said yes to me." He patted his chest then pointed his remote to unlock his car, then helped her inside. "As a matter of fact, I praise God for this moment." Once he was behind the wheel, Marlon whispered a prayer of thanks, then drove off. "I thought I'd take you to Hank's Place in U-City. It has some good soul food."

"You're making me miss my mom's cooking." She stretched her gorgeous legs.

Clearing his throat to tame his building attraction, Marlon asked her take on the message.

"It was powerful and a reminder not to get sidetracked. I thought about my marriage and why it didn't work. Forces in high places were intervening. I wasn't wearing any armor to shield me from the attacks."

Marlon almost slammed on his brakes. "He hit you?" He could feel his nostrils flare.

Portia shook her head. "There's more than one way to wound a person without a physical blow." He relaxed somewhat. "He knew how to crush me—my self-confidence—all because he held my heart."

"I've never hit a woman."

She angled her body and faced him. "I believe you, but you cheated on your wife like Leonard did with me." She paused and seemed to study him. "Sorry to bring it up, but you told me to talk to you, and that bothers me. I'm trying to comprehend the man who seems perfect with a man would who didn't think twice about breaking his vow."

"Trust me, I thought long and hard." Would he ever win this battle? "I'm glad you think I'm perfect—God is tweaking me, according to 1 Corinthians 6:11. Second, my marriage was already broken when I decided to get even. That sounds so crazy for me to say that now." He cringed and gripped the wheel. "I've regretted that decision. Sleeping with another woman who wasn't my wife didn't make me feel victorious, it made me feel like a scum."

"Hey." She reached over and rubbed his arm. The gesture surprised him as well as provided comfort. "I won't bring this up again."

"It took a whole lot of repenting before I had the nerve to step foot in church, and even now, from time to time, God reminds me to believe He forgave me." She quietly listened, rubbing his hand as if saying, it's all right. "I went into my marriage believing in fidelity. I struggled to forgive Tammy the first time she cheated, even after a lot of prayer, the second time was testing me, by the third affair, I lashed out with everything within me to even the score, except I'm the one who hated myself more than she hated me."

It was the trial of your faith, being much more precious than of gold that perishes, though it be tried with fire, might be found unto praise and honor and glory at My appearing, God whispered 1 Peter 1:7.

Thank you, Lord. Marlon glanced at her to gage her reaction, then back at the road. "If a woman could know my past and love me despite my flaws, I would marry her and be faithful to her until my last breath."

"I think there is a woman out there who could do that."

Are you that woman? he wanted to ask, but it was too soon to talk that type of commitment.

In a bold move, testing the waters, he wrapped his hand around one of hers, and she didn't pull back. Their connection felt right.

By the time they reached Hank's Place, he was glad they had cleared the air, removing barriers. After perusing the menu and placing their orders, Portia chose a table that overlooked the patio.

Although it was an unseasonably warm October weekend, it would be too cool outside to enjoy their meal whenever the wind stirred.

Once seated, Marlon admired Portia under the hood of his lashes as she rummaged through her purse. Gorgeous didn't begin to describe her—glossy hair, long lashes, pouty lips and a delicate chin. Her curves accented her shapely legs. She definitely had the physical assets, but it was her heart that was alluring.

"So can we agree that our past marriages are our past, and let's work on building up our strength in Christ along with a friendship in the present?" Marlon pressed her.

"I would like that."

Minutes later, a young server set their meals before them. After thanking him. Portia pulled out hand sanitizer, which she squirted playfully at his hand until he opened his palms. Covering her hands with his, he meticulous cleaned them together.

She blushed, but didn't say anything as he bowed his head to pray. "Lord, in the name of Jesus, we thank You for this fellowship. Bless us, this food, and our families. Remove the impurities and help us to bless those who are hungry in Jesus name. Amen."

No words were exchanged as they sampled their yams, collard greens, smothered pork chops, and more. Portia came up for air first.

"Good, huh?" He grinned as she nodded. "Told ya."

Their conversation was lighthearted. He listened as she talked about Emerald. "My niece has been my best therapy—her innocence, silliness, and carefree living. Sometimes, she climbs in my bed to sleep until Coy gets home. Those simple gestures make me feel so special and important in her life. I'm glad your daughters are in her life."

"Mikaela and Alyssa love her too." He paused, debating whether she would appreciate his honesty directed at her. "And I'm glad you're in mine for whatever will happen between us, but know this Ms. Hunter, I'm attracted to you, too, very much."

"Confession is good for the soul," she teased, barely containing a smile.

So she was in a playful mood? He liked that. "Okay, and I'll be waiting on yours."

The date ended at Coy's doorstep. "Thanks, Marlon. You surprised me," she said, gazing into his mesmerizing brown eyes.

"In what way?" He stepped closer.

"I enjoyed myself." *Why am I surprised?* Their attraction was on the table and so were their wounds, yet despite that, she was happy they had gone out.

"And I enjoyed you." Leaning forward, he

paused as she sucked in her breath. Was he waiting for her permission as he stared into her eyes? Portia froze. When his lips touched hers, it seemed to zap all her strength, then his strong arms engulfed her in a cocoon of warmth. She thought she would faint, but somehow she floated back to reality.

"Oh, wow," she heard herself say before she fluttered her lashes to look at Marlon. "Nice."

"I know. I've been waiting to kiss you since the Hallelujah party."

She blinked still dazed. "The kiss? I was talking about the hug." Portia frowned.

"Woman, you know how to shoot a brother down." He didn't hide his vulnerability.

"The kiss was nice." She smiled. "But the hug…" She paused to relive the moment, and her eyes teared. "I haven't had that in years. My dad's gone, no brothers, and no husband."

Marlon's lips curved upward. "Any time you want a hug, like this—" He pulled her back into his arms, and she snuggled against his chest. "Just ask. I'm available."

CHAPTER TEN

It had been two weeks since Marlon held Portia in his arms and she didn't protest. He had no idea how much that gesture affected her. It was tight, not lusty or weak. The embrace was euphoric, and spiritual, as if he was sharing with her a portion of whatever strength God was giving him.

Their first date had been exhilarating and exhausting—from the church service to a late brunch to gourmet cupcakes from the local favorite Jilly's to a matinee at nearby Galleria. She'd enjoyed every minute of it.

Her smile faded to a slight pout, because obligations kept them apart. Marlon didn't let that sever the relationship they had started to build. Just this morning he'd sent her: Jude 1:24. God can keep us from falling. I want to be kept the next time around.

It was as if he was tapping into her insecurity about his faithfulness, even though she never brought up the conversation again. She missed him.

The calendar changed to November, and Portia's workload was relentless. February, May, and November in the television industry were known as "sweeps". Rival stations' goal was to lure advertisers by scoring the highest ratings on original stories and investigation pieces during the newscasts.

Sweeps were also highly stressful for employees where their focus was being one at breaking news coverage. Portia was brought in to assist with special news projects. Although she was thankful for more hours, it meant helping Coy less. Then there was Marlon.

Portia exhaled and relived the soft good night kiss on her sister's doorstep. Her lips still tingled whenever she thought about it. Her arms shivered every time she recalled the warmth of Marlon's arms. *Jesus, I'm confessing, I like Marlon.*

She blinked to compartmentalize her memories as she sat in an editing booth, reviewing video footage of a recent protest. She had to be on top of her game while waiting for a full-time position. This was not the time to lose sight of her mission.

As she rewound the video, one image stood out. Police, in full riot gear, charged the group of protesters, knocking over an elderly woman in the process. She jotted down the time log. Her heart plummeted. Scenes like this had been replaying across the country after cops were acquitted of killing unarmed black youths and men. The stories were heart-wrenching, but her hope was in heaven where the righteous Judge would never make a mistake on punishing the guilty parties or rewarding the faithful.

Suddenly, her phone alerted her of a text—either

Coy or Marlon. She hoped for the latter. Portia smiled as she read the message.

`Just thinking about you. Don't work too hard. My Proverbs 31:30 woman.`

`I won't. John 3:16,` she texted back, loving the spiritual aspect of their relationship.

While Marlon believed in going overboard for Christmas presents when it came to Mikaela and Alyssa, Portia's Christmas list would be small gifts for her sister, mother, Emerald...and now, Marlon and his girls.

Her mother arrived at St. Louis Lambert Airport the Sunday before Thanksgiving. It had been a tradition for them to spend this holiday together. The last two years of Portia's marriage had been so bad, she didn't have the strength and money to travel to St. Louis or Texas, so her mom, sister, and niece had driven to Kansas City to cheer her up.

"Child, you've gotten taller since the summer," Carol fused over Emerald, smothering her with tight hugs.

"Leave some love for us, Momma," Coy teased before receiving her portion. Portia was last to be smothered with love. After retrieving their mother's luggage, they rode back to Coy's. Carol wasted no time invading the kitchen, getting started on her holiday baking while Portia and Coy apologized that they had to work.

"Don't worry about entertaining me. My grandbaby is going to help me bake cookies and pies…" She winked.

"Yeah!" Emerald's eyes sparkled.

"Mom, don't overdo it again. It's just the four of us."

"Hush, Coy. That's why extra food is called leftovers."

Coy's place felt like home for the holidays with the aromas coming from the kitchen filling the house for days. Surprisingly, Portia didn't have to work on Thanksgiving, but she was on the schedule for Black Friday. Coy had to work on Thanksgiving evening.

The next morning, Emerald was chatting away with her grandmother in the kitchen. "My grandbaby has been telling me stories about Jesus. I'm glad you're going back to church." She wore a pleased expression.

"That's Portia." Coy pointed out, then opened the refrigerator for juice. "I've been working on Sundays."

"I'll pray God changes that." Carol jutted her chin.

"The messages are inspiring," Portia said, taking a seat at the table and grabbing an orange cranberry muffin from a stack.

"And so is Mr. Washington," Coy added with a

smirk and joined Portia at the table.

Emerald's face glowed as she proceeded to tell her grandmother about her best friend Mikaela and her little sister.

Their mother listened intensively until her granddaughter took a breath. "Sweetie, why don't you go play so I can talk to my girls?"

There was a reason why Portia was hush-hush about her relationship with Marlon. Sometimes she was afraid of being too happy, and wondered if she would wake up and it all would be a dream. She exchanged glances with Coy.

After making herself comfortable in a chair, Carol looked at them with a somber expression. "All I want, whether it be this Christmas or next, is for both of my daughters to find happiness. There are good men out there, like your daddy. A man can't find a wife, like Proverbs 18 says, if the woman is hiding. I'm not talking about in plain sight, but her feelings." When Coy was about to speak, Carol shook her head. "Marriage is hard work, and submission to God's will is necessary—for the husband and his wife."

"I submitted my heart, Momma, but Leonard crushed it with his hatred, lies, and infidelity," Portia said softly, but the admission this time didn't hurt the way it used to.

"He didn't submit to God, baby."

Coy folded her arms. "And not when your husband doesn't want to work."

"True. It was Eric's father who was responsible for making a man out of a boy, but you married him, because you loved him, and you can love again. Stop hiding behind your fearless armor. God created males and females to be married and companions. You don't have to go solo." She turned to Portia. "I heard quite a bit from Emerald. Now, I want to hear from you about this Marlon Washington."

Portia blushed. "I like him, and I didn't think I would." She frowned to find the words. "I'm enjoying the spiritual journey we're on together."

"Then I like him already." Her mother patted the table, then stood. "I expect to meet him while I'm here. That isn't a request."

It wasn't going to happen this Thanksgiving morning. Not only had Marlon overslept, but from the looks of his daughters, Mikaela and Alyssa needed more attention: baths, hair, food, and clothes, then they had to make it across town in a half hour for church.

He thought about Portia. She was probably there soaking up the message without him. That seemed to be their meeting place when she wasn't working. At least when she wasn't available for dinner, they could dine together on the Word.

Getting up, Marlon reflected on all the things he was thankful for, so he knelt and prayed. When he stayed too long on his knees, the girls came into his room. While he supervised Mikaela's cooking them breakfast of rice, eggs, and bacon, his mother called to see what time he was coming over.

"Around one. Oh, and Mom, do you have an extra pie I can take?"

"I always have extra food for my sons."

Growing up, Marlon and his brothers didn't enjoy the holidays as much when they had to divide their time between their home and their father's place. Today was no different with his girls. His two younger brothers who lived out of town had flown in for day were at his mother's house when he and the girls arrived. Plus, Derek and his family were there, along with Robyn's mother. The house was loud, busy and the way his mother enjoyed it, full of life. His phone alerted him of a text. It was Portia.

Missed you at service earlier.

I've been missing you period, Marlon texted back. He craved seeing Portia. After a respectable amount of time catching up with his brothers and going back for seconds, Marlon gathered his girls to go to his dad's house.

Mikaela and Alyssa weren't happy about leaving Derek and little Deborah. When he told them where their last stop would be, they grabbed their coats and met him at the door to the amusement of all the adults.

"Tell Portia I'll call her," Robyn said before he gave his final goodbyes.

Marlon reached his destination to the city thirty minutes later. Once he helped his girls out of the car, he held their hands and climbed the stairs. His father met them at the door. "There's my princesses." He lifted them into the air. "Hey, son." Tyrone released them and shook Marlon's hand.

His father's third wife, Janice, walked out the kitchen and greeted them. The girls and Marlon declined eating another bite. When she offered dessert, Mikaela blurted out. "We have Grandma's apple pie in the car."

Tyrone's face brightened. Although his wife was a decent cook, she couldn't beat Lane Washington when it came to desserts.

"We've got one more stop to make, and it's going with us," Marlon explained as his father didn't hide his disappointment.

Marlon knew his father had regrets about his life, and he often lectured Derek and Marlon about the repercussions of ruining good marriages. He was beyond ecstatic when Derek and Robyn remarried. Tyrone blamed himself for turning his younger sons against the idea of marriage. Bryson and Austin, both in their late twenties, wanted no part of being a husband.

"We're going to see my best friend and her aunt, Ms. Portia. She's pretty, Grandpa."

Tyrone gave Marlon a side glance. Whatever he was thinking momentarily had him speechless. "If she's a good woman, don't mess it up."

Marlon felt sorry for his dad who didn't lead by example to show his four sons how to be a good husband. He did, however, give them a clear picture of what settling in an okay marriage looked like.

Janice coaxed the girls into the kitchen for cookies and milk. She was a sweet woman without any children of her own and doted on the Washington grandchildren. For about an hour, Marlon watched a football game with his dad before announcing it was time for him and the girls to leave.

Once he was in the car, he texted Portia. Can I invite myself and the girls over?

Open invitation. :)

That was all he needed to know. On our way. I have the girls.

See you soon. Be safe, okay?

Okay, he whispered to himself. Knowing that another woman, who wasn't his mother, or daughters, cared about him made everything seem all right in his world. The girls had dozed, but Mikaela woke instantly when the car stopped, then nudged her sister. "Wake up, Ally."

Portia opened the door before he could knock twice. As he stared at her face, it seemed like forever and ever since they had spent time together. "I've missed you," he whispered, stepping inside as Emerald ran to the door and dragged his daughters away. He handed over his pie.

Portia accepted with a suspicious lift of an eyebrow. "Please tell me you didn't bake this like you made the soup. Even I struggle with homemade crust."

"My mom."

"Well, good evening, young man." An older and shorter version of Portia appeared out of the kitchen. She extended her hand. "I'm Carol."

He was about to shake her hand, but she reached for the pie. "I hope it's apple, because I made peach cobbler."

"It is." He chuckled to himself.

The woman squinted and scrutinized him. "So you're Mr. Washington, the one who makes my daughter's eyes sparkle." Portia bowed her head in embarrassment. "Let's go in the kitchen, so I can get to know you better over a slice of pie."

Marlon took Portia's hand and squeezed it. She squeezed back, and the electric current seemed to flow between them as they trailed her mother. Pans and covered dishes graced the stove and counters, but the table was clutter-free.

He pulled out the chair for Portia, then Carol, once she retrieved a knife and saucers.

"So, what would you like me to know about you?"

He shifted in his seat. "I'm thirty-eight, a divorced father of two adorable, beautiful little girls. I'm gainfully employed as an electrician..." He continued rambling off the basics before facing Portia. "...and thank you for creating such a beautiful woman inside and out."

Carol smiled. "So tell me one thing you *don't* want me to know." She was a dainty eater as she forked off a section, then guided the morsel in her mouth, never taking her eyes off him.

Startled by the question, he stuttered, "Ah, I think my life is an open book."

"Good, then I won't have to dig deep to find any dirt." She shrugged.

"Mom," Portia began, but her mother ignored the interruption.

"As the father of those sweet little girls, I'm sure that gives insight on a mother's love. Portia is my mini-me. When she was hurting, so did I. I don't want her hurt again."

He nodded. "It's a myth that men don't get hurt in relationships. I bled too in my marriage."

Carol nodded. "Yes, I imagine so, but my

daughter's wound isn't completely closed, so she's susceptible to infections and re-injury. I can't let that happen again." She leaned over the table. "I won't. If you're not serious about her, walk away."

The lioness had spoken, and he respected that, but he was a lion. "No man, knowing the value of a precious jewel, or antique throws it away. I may not be the Great Physician as Jesus is, but I plan to apply ointment, bandages, or whatever else she needs to heal."

"Good answer." She lifted her chin, and added, "And good pie, too, by the way."

This time, Marlon snickered. "I'll send your compliments to my mother." He turned to Portia. "Want to catch a movie? I can have my mother babysit."

Carol cleared her throat. "Am I not sitting here? You two go." She stood and shooed them out of the kitchen. "Remember, Marlon, I'm expecting a whole lot from you. Don't disappoint me."

CHAPTER ELEVEN

"She likes you," Portia said once they were settled in his car.

Marlon reached over and squeezed her hand. "I wasn't sure. "How can you tell?"

"You're honesty is like a fresh haircut. A person can't help but see it." They made it to the theater in no time. Inside, she eyed the crowd and frowned. "Are you sure you want to wait in this long line?"

When he gazed into her eyes, she felt like they were the only two people in the lobby, or the world. Nothing else around them mattered. Not only did she feel physically secure with him, but she trusted him to protect her emotions.

"It's been torture wanting to see you all day, but we had to do the family protocol. I want an encore of our first date." He gave her a boyish grin. He was so cute and handsome at the same time.

"Our marathon date?" Portia batted her lashes. She couldn't believe she was flirting?

"And it made up for all the times I wanted to take you out. I'll run a relationship marathon with you any time," he said softly, squeezing her closer as they inched forward.

"I have to work in the morning, so I think this movie is my limit tonight."

The line moved fast and soon Marlon stood in

another line to get her bottled water and popcorn.

Once they were settled in their seats, Portia's lids slowly drifted a few minutes into the movie. She didn't realize she and Marlon had fallen asleep until others were climbing over them to exit the theater.

Marlon stirred and stretched. They both faced each other, blinked, and laughed. He was the first to apologize. "I'm sorry. When I looked over and saw you dozing, I closed my eyes for a minute. I guess the minute turned into an hour and a half. I'm a sorry date, huh?"

She smiled and touched his hand. "Hey, you're also a father of two very active girls. You work all day and still manage to be a great dad."

His eyes seemed to soften at her compliments. "I'm the bad date." She patted her chest. "I don't even have children to be exhausted."

He linked his fingers through hers. "But you're working hard and helping your sister with Emerald. That qualifies as a full plate."

She twisted her lips. "It's more like Coy is helping me rebuild my life. She's not charging me room or board, but I do help with groceries and other things."

Marlon stood and pulled her to her feet, then wrapped his arms around her. She snuggled in his embrace and closed her eyes. She was content, listening to his breathing while breathing in his cologne. She could never get enough of feeling secure, cherished and loved. Love? She opened her eyes. The thought startled her. Portia stepped back shaken. *Lord, is this love?* Questions swirled as Marlon's voice drew her back into the present. "Next Saturday, it's you and me. If you don't have to work, please don't."

"I don't have the luxury of requesting off days, except when I had the flu. Otherwise, I don't turn down hours."

"I'll take care of the shortage. You won't regret saying yes." He tugged her closer by her sweater and brushed his lips against hers—it was so brief. Either it was meant as a tease, or he wasn't sure of his boundaries with her. "Now, about the movie. What was your favorite part?"

Laughing, Portia elbowed him before stepping into the aisle and walking down the steps to the exit. Marlon was by her side with a firm but soft hold on her back to keep her from slipping.

She might not fall physically, but she had already fallen for him.

Portia was counting down the days until her second dating marathon with Marlon. She felt giddy as she sat across the table from Robyn, enjoying a mouthful of chili on her lunch break.

They chatted about everything until Robyn cleared her throat. "I'm just going to put it out there. I was wrong about you and my brother-in-law."

Uh-oh. A bad feeling dropped to the pit of Portia's stomach. She slowly rested her spoon in the bowl. *God, can my heart withstand another heartache?* She swallowed and waited.

"I overheard Derek teasing Marlon about his feelings for you." Robyn smiled. "Marlon said you had his heart in a way his first wife never had, and that he trusted you with it."

Portia exhaled, relieved that it wasn't something devastating. Once she relaxed, her heart fluttered.

"I actually warned Marlon to stay away from you."

"Why?" Portia's heart did a flip-flop and began to pound wildly. So it was Robyn who wasn't genuine?

Tapping her fingers on the table, Robyn leaned forward. "When we first met, I sensed you were still hurting from your divorce. Although my brother-in-law had finally recovered from his, I was concerned for both of you—if you were on the same page. I didn't want to see either of you get hurt, but seeing you two together now, I feel both of you were meant for each other."

Portia exhaled again and gave her friend a smile.

"Thanks for having my back, but I grieved until my divorce was final. After that, I've been in recovery mode."

"Has the doctor released you from His care?" Robyn grinned.

"Let's just say Marlon Washington isn't a man I could keep at arm's length." They agreed with high fives, and Portia chuckled. "During the divorce process, I had a resolve like Coy. One marriage is enough, because 'I hate all men.' I was in a bad place where I even lashed out at God, mad at Him for what someone else did to me." She sighed and glanced out the window, ashamed of the way she had dishonored the Lord. "Now, Jude 1:20 is in full force in my life."

Robyn tilted her head from side to side, then asked, "I know Jude 1:24 by memory. What does verse twenty say that I need to apply to my life?"

" *'Beloved, building up yourselves on your most holy faith, praying in the Holy Ghost,'* has become Marlon and my favorite Scripture." She paused as her mind drifted. "You know, on the day of my divorce, Leonard sat in the courtroom with his girlfriend, smiling as if he had a new pair of dentures. The last I heard was that he was getting remarried. It was as if he was taunting his happiness. That moment was a turning point in my life where I refused to be miserable with or without him."

Robyn nodded. "Sometimes happiness is the best revenge to your ex., but Derek and I could never be happy without each other." She had a whimsical expression. "It took years apart for us to realize that. Marlon is a good guy."

"I know." She blushed, "I admire the way he loves on Mikaela and Alyssa, yet is firm with them. At first, his honesty about his past turned me off, but it's because of his honesty, I feel free to be me."

"I guess his looks didn't have anything to do with it." Robyn grinned.

Portia laughed. "His looks had a whole lot to do with it." They exchanged high fives. Their lunch ended too soon, so they said their goodbyes and went back to work.

On Thursday morning, a few days into December, St. Louis got its first day of significant snowfall for the season. School was canceled. It worked out that Portia was off, so they would be snowed in together.

Unfortunately, Coy was stuck at work until her relief could get there. Portia and Emerald remained in their jammies in front of the gas fireplace until it was almost noon, playing checkers after Portia had gotten whipped in a video game with Emerald.

Suddenly, they heard thumps against the window. Emerald scrambled to her feet and went to investigate. She giggled. When Portia peeked outside, she laughed too.

Marlon yelled from the front yard. His girls were in the background. "Can you come out and play?"

"Can we?" Emerald pleaded, jumping in place with a hopeful expression.

"Sure." Portia mustered up her best game face at Marlon and mouthed, "It's on."

Turning from the window, she and her niece raced to their rooms to change. "Emerald, make sure you put on extra pants and T-shirts. I don't want you sick."

"Okay," she yelled back.

Upstairs, in her loft bedroom, Portia did the same. Before stepping outside, she double-checked that her niece was insulated like a polar bear. "Ready?"

"Yeah!" She grinned.

Opening the door, a wet snowball kissed Portia in the face. Emerald laughed as Portia wiped away the moisture. She bobbed her head at the culprit. "Okay, Mr. Washington. I'm going to pay you back for that."

She helped Emerald off the porch and noticed it and walkway had been cleared. The snowplow had made a path on the street, but the shovel against Marlon's car was the evidence of his personal touch. If Derek was anything like his big brother, Portia could see why Robyn couldn't live without him. Marlon was a prince. Mikaela and Alyssa were forming a snowman, so her niece headed in that direction.

Marlon stood a few feet away bouncing a snowball in his hand. He wore a down jacket, work boots, a fur-lined cap and a smirk. Mischief danced in his eyes.

Portia leaned down to gather snow for retaliation and a snowball hit her. The girls laughed as Marlon acted as if he hadn't moved. Standing, she rolled the ball in her gloved hand, then marched in his direction. Inches from him, Portia took the snow and rubbed it in his face. "There, take that!"

Spitting the snow out of his mouth, he suddenly snaked his arm around her waist, then lifted her off her feet before she could blink.

"Woman, is that all you've got?" Nestled safely in his arms, he twirled her around as she squealed. When was the last time she played in snow? It was coming down heavy, adding to the foot already on the ground.

"Don't you drop me!" she warned.

Marlon grinned. "I'd never drop you," he said huskily as he placed her in the snow. Then laughed.

Scrambling to her feet, she gathered snowballs and began to chase him around the yard. The girls abandoned their snowman and joined her team as the four-against-one game was on. Finally, out of breath, Portia called a truce, huffing. The girls returned to their snowman and Marlon to her side.

"I love you, Portia. I know you're still healing. I want to help close the wound."

Speechless, she stared at him, not expecting such a serious declaration during playtime. She stuttered, "I don't know what to say."

"Say you know, say you believe me, say..." Even with the snow coming down and blinding them, she didn't miss the intensity in his eyes. "I want you to know where my mind is and who has my heart." He took her gloved hand and placed it on his chest. "When you told me not to drop you, I had to let you know I won't."

Portia was speechless. She knew without a doubt that he loved her. Was she ready to make such a bold—can't take back—declaration? Their attraction had been building since September, and now three months later, it was undeniably strong, yet, he loved her? She blinked. In all honesty, love was on the tip of her tongue, but she questioned her emotions to confess it. "I don't know how long it's going to take me to say it back, or...if I will." She bowed her head.

He took her hand and squeezed it. "I have no doubt you will, because our feelings are pure."

Marlon was about to make her cry, and once she

started, Portia doubted she would be able to stop. Nodding, she turned and looked at the girls for a distraction. "Who wants some stew and hot chocolate?"

"Me!" the trio sang.

Inside, Portia gave the girls a change of clothes, then put theirs in the dryer while Marlon removed his boots.

After devouring the stew and cups of hot chocolate, the girls raced off to play in Emerald's room. When she thought they were alone, Mikaela returned with Alyssa trailing, and hugged her. Closing her eyes, she soaked up their love. Not only did their daddy give good hugs, theirs were just a warm. Portia kissed them on their cheeks as Emerald summoned them back to her room.

She glanced at Marlon and he looked at her as if he knew how sentimental that moment had been. He stood and reached for her hand. "Come."

Latching on to him, they strolled into the living room and relaxed in front of the fire. Marlon was quiet, allowing her to process her emotions and replay his "confession" in her head. Every first snowfall of the season she would always remember him telling her he loved her. Rubbing her arms, Portia could feel his eyes on her. After clearing her throat, she whispered, "Are you sure?"

"I have no doubt my feelings for you," he

answered as if they were in the middle of the earlier conversation.

"Why?"

He smirked. "Was that supposed to be a trick question? I've fallen hard for you, because you're gorgeous, stunning, and exotic on the outside, and beautiful, sweet, and pure on the inside. That is a million dollar combination. I want you to know I'm here for you."

She frowned. "What if I never love you back?"

He squinted. "I dare you not to love me." The challenge was unmistakable.

Portia shivered. If this was a bet, she was sure to lose.

CHAPTER TWELVE

Saturday morning, Marlon rolled over in bed and grabbed his phone, then paused. Closing his eyes, he thanked God for another day and for a second chance at love. Portia loved him. He was sure of it, so now he had to wait to hear it from her. "Lord, help me to be patient." Opening his eyes, he proceeded to text her. `Ready for another dating marathon?`

Minutes later, she answered back. `Yes...I'm excited.`

He grinned, imagining her smile. `See you soon, babe.`

Yes, he had taken the liberty with the endearment, because there was no turning back. Sliding on his knees, he prayed again. "Lord, in the name of Jesus, let Your perfect will be done in my life."

There used to be a time, he was weary of God's will, but with, or without Portia in his life, he would keep a steady pace on the narrow road to please God. "I hope Portia is a part of it, but we're both trusting You. Thank You for so much for everything—my children and even their mother."

Tammy made it clear when she was released, she would marry her lover, Jeffrey Somebody. He ended his petition in Jesus' name, then got up to begin his day. After waking the girls, he returned to his room for one hundred pushups before jumping in the shower.

When he strolled into the kitchen, Mikaela was dumping fruit into the blender. Alyssa was nearby with a fist full of blueberries, handing them to her sister. Neither of them were dressed, nor their hair combed. Whether their faces were washed was also questionable. "What are you two doing?"

"Making a smoothie like Ms. Portia showed me at the slumber party."

Alyssa nodded. "I'm helping."

Marlon did his best to keep a straight face as he ushered them out of the kitchen, so they could start their morning "beauty" rituals. He smiled. His family was rooting for him and Portia to be an exclusive couple. Marlon had more than enough offers for babysitting, even from his father and his third wife, since they had yet to meet her.

There wouldn't be any introductions today. Marlon planned to be selfish with her. To give his mother a rest, he was going to drop the girls off at his brother's, where Robyn always made chocolate chip pancakes when her nieces spent the night.

"Mikaela, do you have your suitcase—"

"Yes, Daddy. I packed Ally's stuffed animal and mine too, and our dresses for church today. We're ready." She grinned.

"You mean tomorrow, my lovely. Today's Saturday, remember?" Their thick, wavy hair still begged for attention. He would let his sister-in-law handle that. Putting caps on their heads, he said, "Let's go."

Less than ten minutes later, Robyn greeted them at her door. After hugs, his daughters made a beeline for Tyler and his toddler sister, Deborah, who the girls still called a baby.

Robyn frowned at the girls' hair. "I hope your next child is a boy," she teased.

"Me too."

"Hey, where's Emerald?" she asked.

"I'm going to get her and Portia now."

"You know, you could have done this in one trip." She shook her head. "Men."

Portia wasn't sure how she should dress for an all-day date on a cold weekend. When Emerald gave her the thumbs up, Portia decided her black sweater dress, leggings and colorful scarf passed inspection. She also layered her look. She could be cute, but she wasn't freezing for anybody as she slipped her sock-covered feet into knee-high boots.

"And see, you almost said no to Marlon and yes to work," Coy said a few days earlier when she was making lunch for herself and Emerald.

"Technically, I did call to work, but they didn't need me after all."

"Sis, love is hard to find the first time. This time, let love find you, like Mom said. You can stay here as long as you'd like, or..." Coy paused. *"Until Marlon has other plans."*

At the time her sister had said that, Coy had no idea Marlon had professed his love. She finger-combed her hair as the bell rang. Her heart pounded at seeing Marlon again.

Emerald had her suitcase in her hand. Portia was excited too. She craved Marlon's hugs. They were strong, but gentle. He didn't disappoint when she opened the door. "Hi." The embrace was swift, but lasting as he escorted her and Emerald to his car.

At Robyn's house, Portia thanked her.

"Girl, please. I believe in happy endings. 'Tis the season to be married—merry. Get it?"

Back in Marlon's car, she joked, "I feel like I'm married with children and escaping."

"I'll be glad to share the experience with you." He reached for her hand and squeezed it, then winked. "Now, crepes, French toast, pancakes?"

She tapped her lips, thinking. "Crepes—first choice, then Belgian waffles."

"Scape American Bistro in the Central West End won't disappoint."

Portia watched as Marlon bobbed his head. He

was such a strong, but sensitive handsome man with a good heart. What woman wouldn't want the ultimate package?

He glanced her way. "What's going through your head? The truth, tell me," he said, then looked back at the road as he exited on I-64.

Shifting in her seat, she faced him. "How could your wife walk away when she had everything?"

He grunted. "That's the same question I asked myself when I learned you were divorced."

Portia nodded. "Since you put it that way, I know the answer's complicated."

"And our past is off limits today. I want you and me to create good memories. Agree?"

"Yes." He was right. The less she thought about her former marriage, the more she could live again.

During the ride from Kirkwood to the restaurant on Maryland Avenue, Portia enjoyed easy conversation. She was loved, even if he didn't say it, and felt no pressure for anything deep or a heart-to-heart. They discussed growing up, hobbies, and the girls. She giggled at one point.

"What?" Marlon chuckled and squeezed her hand.

"I talk about Emerald as if she's my child instead of my niece."

Exiting onto Kingshighway, they bypassed Barnes-Jewish and Children's Hospital that was a landmark off the highway. The Central West End was home to many residents with "old money", living in imposing mansions that lined Lindell Boulevard and other private streets. The old mixed with a thriving community of millennials who preferred spacious condos. Once Marlon parked at a meter, he came around to her door and helped her out.

A feeling of contentment descended on Portia, and she wanted to scream her happiness. In lieu of drawing attention, she contained herself as she and Marlon wrapped an arm around each other's waists and trekked across the street.

For the next hour, they forced fed each other samples from their plates. It brought back memories of his tenderness when she was sick. Did he love her then?

"Well," he said, patting his stomach, "we can burn off some calories at Steinburg Rink, if you're up to ice skating."

"I haven't ice skated in years." The outdoor ice rink in Forest Park was a favorite attraction to locals and visitors. As soon as the season opened, the rink was packed with skaters, and onlookers too.

Marlon signaled the waiter for their check. "Unless you think it's too cold, want to skate a few rounds?"

"Sure. I think I'm dressed warm enough for the

elements."

In no time, they were lacing up their skates. With her hands in both of his, Portia let him guide her on the ice until she was steady on her feet. "I'm impressed."

He did a slight bow. "Thank you, madam."

"I meant me." She giggled. "I've still got it, and you're pretty good too." She was about to take off, but Marlon was faster and trapped around her waist with one arm.

"My daughters are better than me. I try to experience things with them, at least once. You know, the more we're together, I'm amused by your sense of humor. I like it."

"Thank you for allowing me to be me," she said softly as they found their rhythm and skated as one.

After an hour, they called it quits. Back inside Marlon's car, he blasted the heat until she thawed.

"Now, are you a shopper? 'Tis the season to brave the stores."

Portia smirked, recalling how Robyn had feigned a slip of the tongue with 'tis the season to be married.' She chuckled, then glanced out the window and sobered. "Shopping used to be my favorite pastime. Now, I'm frugal with my money, not knowing when and how many hours I'll—"

"Hey," he said, guiding her chin to his face, "no, bad memories, remember? I have something for you." He reached into his pocket and pulled out an envelope.

"What's this?" She frowned, hesitant to take it. Portia stared at it, then him.

"A gift. You didn't tell me whether you were scheduled off work or not, but I'm glad you're here with me, so please accept this."

She swallowed. So he was serious about paying her to take off for their date? She was speechless as she processed that until finally, she said, "I can't."

"Open it before you reject my gift."

When he looked wounded, she did as he asked. The greeting card had an image of a woman with her eyes closed. She had dainty lashes. Opening the card, she spied a gift card, then met his eyes. "Thank you."

"You're welcome. Now, you do have spending money." He grinned.

"Exactly how much is this?" She eyed him suspiciously. It might not be cash, but that didn't mean he didn't try to compensate for it in a gift card.

"Hey, I take offense!" He mocked insult. "A woman doesn't want a man asking her if the hair on her head was purchased over a counter or given at birth."

She fingered her locks. "This is my God-given hair." She playfully *hmph*ed. "What does my hair have to do with this card?"

"It's a touchy issue, and for the record, it

wouldn't matter to me. Your beauty isn't defined by your hair," he said softly, sincerely. "Well, I don't want my gifts to be a touchy subject with you either, whether it's in the form of a gift card, dinner, or anything else. Plus, I'm not telling." "She wrinkled her nose at him and enjoyed the half hour drive on I-64 toward Chesterfield Mall. When Marlon passed the exit, she turned to him. "Where are we going?"

"I thought you would like the Premium Outlets."

Note to self: this man loves the cold weather: snowball, ice skating and shopping outdoors, bypassing three indoors malls to get there. She loved cold weather too, as long as she was bundled up.

When they arrived and parked, the couple walked hand in hand to the directory to see what stores they would hit. "Do you want or need anything?" he asked.

Spiritual blessings came to mind, but Portia shook her head on the materialistic category. "I might have given away or sold most of my possessions, but all my clothes, I brought with me. "What about you?"

"Nah. I'm a simple man—"

"There's nothing simple about you, Marlon Washington," she said, patting his arm and an idea came to her, "but since I have some play money, let's dress you today."

"Me?" He laughed. "This should be interesting."

Marlon wrapped his arm around her waist, and Portia leaned into him as they began their stroll. The Brooks Brothers Factory Store was their first stop. She was soon convinced bright colors—red, royal blue, and mustard yellow enhanced his dark skin tone. Before leaving the store, he purchased two sweaters only because she said she liked them. For some unknown reason, his gesture seemed to empower her.

Continuing their mission, the couple window-shopped until kid stores came into view and they went inside. She battled a bout of melancholy. Portia always dreamed of her and her hubby going shopping for their children. She was quiet as they scanned the clothes racks.

"Hey," Marlon said softly, reminding her of his presence. "What's one thing you would like to have for Christmas?"

Besides a family of my own? she mused, then shrugged. "God's gifts aren't limited to one day of the year, but a full-time job would be nice."

He stilled his movements and touched her hand. "I've been praying that God grants you the desires of your heart—a job, and I hope I'm somewhere on your list."

Portia smiled. She was wondering when he might say something about her unspoken desire.

"I'm just throwing that out there."

"Hmm-mm. Let's finish shopping for the girls, but I'm using my own money for their gifts." Thinking about Emerald, Portia texted her sister to see if her niece needed or wanted anything.

Interesting. ☺ You and Mr. Washington are doing the family thing. Emerald can use the basics— underwear, socks, and pajamas.

Got it, Portia texted back. BTW, I'm sticking out my tongue at you. She laughed. While she picked through items for her niece, she kept a running total of expenses. "I'd better stop."

"You could always use that plastic card I gave you." He wiggled an eyebrow.

"Nah. Don't want to max out my twenty dollar limit," she teased.

"If you're fishing for the amount on the card, I'm still not breaking under the pressure of your pouty lips and seductive eyes. Nope." He shook his head. "I'm not caving into your intoxicating perfume or sweetness. Nope."

Laughing, she playfully elbowed him. Being with Marlon felt natural as if they had known each other for years instead of months. If the gift card was supposed to be a bribe to spend time with him, he could save his money. Portia wouldn't miss another date.

Finally, when Portia hinted that she had enough of the chaos and crowds of Christmas shoppers, Marlon suggested an early dinner at a nearby Italian restaurant. "And I'll even let you select a movie for afterward."

The ambiance at dinner was soothing as a massage. Portia was so relaxed she flirted with smiles and he replied with smothering stares and seductive winks. They finished their meals by sampling each other's dishes.

The sun had begun to set as they exited the theater. "I love the Christmas lights." She slipped her arm through his on the way back to his vehicle.

"Then let's cap off our date with a ride through the annual Winter Wonderland."

Tilles Park, a popular destination during the holidays boasted more than a million lights that twinkled from different scenes throughout the park. Once there, instead of driving, Marlon opted for a carriage ride.

Too soon, their date ended at Coy's door. Marlon cupped her cheeks in his hands and guided her closer to his lips. Even though the air between them was cold, his warm lips nibbled on hers until they were warm too. "I love you," he whispered.

The way her heart succumbed to him, the words were so close to rolling off her lips, but fear held her captive.

Faith overcomes fear, God whispered.

Her lashes fluttered as he stepped back and chuckled. "I do love you. Open the door, and I'll place these bags inside so you can lock up."

Her heart protested that she return his sentiments. Her lips demanded more. One day, she swallowed, one day her faith in herself and this relationship was going to change everything. But not today as she mumbled, "Good night." From the window, Portia watched as Marlon drove off. This time she whispered for her ears only, "I think I'm falling in love with you too."

Emerald and Alyssa were already asleep, but Mikaela had one more thing to do. Her Sunday school teacher had talked about being consistent and confident when praying like the widow in the Bible. "Jesus," she mumbled, "I think my daddy likes Ms. Portia. Please make Ms. Portia like my daddy a lot. She's nice...."

The widow troubled the unjust judge to do her bidding. I am a righteous Judge and I see your faith when you pray. God whispered, the story is in Luke 18.

Mikaela's eyes popped open and she grinned. "Thank You, Jesus. Amen." She scrambled inside her sleeping bag and drifted off to the sleep.

CHAPTER THIRTEEN

Sunday morning, Coy greeted Marlon when he knocked on her front door. He wasn't surprised Portia's sister was on her way out to work.

"Thank you," she said in a low voice as she ushered him inside.

"For what?" Marlon whispered back as he untangled the scarf from around his neck.

She gave him a "duh" expression that reminded him of the way Mikaela looked when the answer was obvious. "Making my sister smile, happy, glow." She glanced toward the kitchen, prompting him to look over his shoulder. "For the past couple of years, she was barely on life support."

Marlon puffed his chest out in pride at the compliment. Before he could thank her, she stopped him.

"But—" Coy put on her game face—"I will personally crush your bones if you hurt her—all two hundred and six of them."

"Yikes." He held up his hands. "I love her. If anyone tries to hurt her, they will answer to me." He patted his chest.

"That's a good answer." She nodded as Portia appeared. As Coy had said and Marlon had already known, Portia's face glowed. Hers eyes sparkled when she noticed he was wearing the blue turtleneck sweater.

"You wore it." She seemed pleased.

"Of course." He stepped closer, towering over her, remembering their kiss the previous night. "You picked it out for me." His nostrils flared and her fragrance tickled his nose.

Coy said her goodbyes and slipped out the door as he made his way to Portia, engulfed her in his arms, and brushed a kiss on her mouth.

"Good morning." Stepping back, he assessed her appearance. She had on a sassy hat that highlighted her gold top and skirt. Today, ankle boots kept her feet snug. "You look beautiful."

She blushed, then reached for her coat, purse and Bible. He took everything except for her handbag.

"How about dinner after church? We can take the girls to a buffet."

"They would enjoy that and so would I."

On the drive to Holy Ghost Temple, they chatted about their favorite holiday dishes, the big stories her station was covering, and of course, the girls. Portia talked about Emerald as if she was a daughter instead of a niece.

They held hands all the way, and after he parked on the church lot, he didn't want to sever their connection. Outside his car, Marlon waited while she slipped her hands back into the gloves, then he secured it in his and strolled toward the entrance. "I missed my girls, even if it was one night."

"I miss them too when they're not with Emerald. I'm not a very good playmate substitute." They continued their stride. "Did I ever tell you that you're a great dad? Mikaela and Alyssa adore you."

He choked at her compliment. He squeezed her hand in appreciation when he'd much rather kiss her. Once they were inside the foyer, he searched in both directions for his little lovelies. "Hmm. Maybe, they're not here yet."

After a few "Good mornings" and "Praise the Lords," they made it to the sanctuary where Robyn, Derek, and the children were indeed seated. How his sister-in-law managed to get three extra little people ready and be on time for church was mind-boggling.

Mikaela must have sensed his presence, because when she turned around, excitement washed over her face.

"You've been spotted," Portia teased.

As they strolled to the pew, Derek stood to shake his hand, then stepped out in the aisle, so he and Portia could enter. His girls jumped up to hug him, and even his niece and nephew vied for his attention. They were chatterboxes before he could take his seat. Then his daughters hugged Portia. He wasn't the only one who fell in love with her. Mikaela and Alyssa were drawn to Portia too.

"Hi, Auntie," Emerald said, grinning and waving. "Hi, Mr. Washington."

It was a good thing the praise team was leading the congregation in songs because the children's whispers were loud. The seating on pew shifted when he created an opening between Alyssa and Mikaela. Emerald squeezed herself between her best friend and Portia. After they knelt and offered a prayer of thanks for being in the Lord's midst again, they took their seats almost in sync. Spiritually, they were getting in sync with God, and maybe it would be a matter of time until their hearts would beat as one.

"Stop focusing on the darkness of the night," their pastor's sermon had Portia riveted. "Psalm 27 and Psalm 30 are two passages you should recite when your heart is heavy. Joy will come—it's not a 'maybe' or a 'might'—but it will come as sure as God told us to wait for the Holy Ghost, because it came and is still being manifested in the saints."

The years of agony, mourning her husband and a crumbling marriage, Portia never imagined a beam of light would pierce her darkness, but here she was content and full of joy as Christmas approached. Portia couldn't explain the happiness blossoming within her, but the seed had been planted. She turned, and Marlon was staring at her as if he was aware of her thoughts.

"You can choose to be happy in life, but only God's joy is a promise. As we're about to celebrate Jesus' birth, think about the gifts He brought to His own party—salvation, joy, blessings, eternal life…" Pastor Kinder's list was endless as he pumped the church. Soon, he extended an invitation for sinners to repent.

"There's also a promise of salvation. To cash in on that promise, God calls for every sinner to repent, footnote, we're all born in sin, so don't think you're exempt. Walk down this aisle for prayer and consent to the water baptism in Jesus' name. Acts 2:39 says, *'For the promise is unto you, and to your children, and to all that are afar off, even as many as the Lord our God shall call.'* Come on and get your gift today. Jesus will redeem you…"

Dozens responded as many filed to the front. The service ended on a high note with baptisms. Plus, God had filled many of them with His Holy Ghost and spoke to them with heavenly tongues.

By the time the benediction was given, Portia felt refreshed. "Wow."

Marlon's eyes sparkled. "Awesome message. Thank you, Jesus, for saving me." Next he reached for his daughters' coats and zipped them up. When Portia was about to grab Emerald's, he saved her from the task. Her niece soaked up the attention.

She silently prayed, "Lord, Your Word says You are a Father to the fatherless, Emerald needs a father—a daddy to show her how she should expect to be treated…"

"Ready?" Marlon pulled her away from her petition with her coat waiting for her to slip it on.

Before leaving the sanctuary, Robyn pulled her aside. "How was the date?"

"It hasn't ended." Portia exhaled. "Honestly, I don't want it to end."

"Good to know," Marlon said, sneaking up behind her.

She giggled from his breath tickling her ear, and Robyn mouthed they would talk later.

"How are you, dear?" Mrs. Washington joined them and asked. "I'm so glad you stole my son and grandbabies' hearts. I stopped counting the number of times they reminded me their daddy was on a date with Ms. Portia, as if they had made reservations for you two." She chuckled.

Portia's eyes teared, humbled by the woman's kind words.

"Are you both coming to the house for an early dinner?" Derek asked, circling his arm around Robyn's waist.

Marlon declined for both them. "No, I'm taking these ladies out to eat."

The girls jumped up and down, jubilant, as if they hadn't been together for the past twenty-four hours.

In the parking lot, Marlon transferred the girls' suitcases from Derek's trunk to his. Once everyone was strapped in, he secured Portia's soft hand in his and gave it a gentle squeeze, then drove toward the restaurant.

What a difference a day made. Yesterday, it had just been her and Marlon, enjoying a romantic dinner. Now, as their table was lively with discussion of Christmas toys, and the fun they had over the weekend. Portia couldn't decide, which scenario she enjoyed more, having Marlon's undivided attention, or sharing it with the girls. It was a tie. Yeah, Portia had fallen in love, because she could see herself as a mother and wife.

CHAPTER FOURTEEN

On Christmas Day, Marlon watched the joy on his daughters' faces as they opened their gifts from the electronics, clothes, and toys.

"Thank you, Daddy," Mikaela said and hugged him. Alyssa followed.

"Don't forget to thank Jesus for His gifts," he said, reminding them that the union job the Lord blessed him with made it possible for them to have things.

"Thank you, Jesus," they said in unison.

Next, he handed them identical gift wrapped boxes. "This is from Ms. Portia."

Mikaela and Alyssa's eyes widened as if their pupils had been dilated. He was with her when she purchased the foldable ballerina flats that had their matching carrying pouches. The box sizes more than accommodated those. He grinned as they ripped apart the paper, then lifted the box top. Alyssa screamed her delight, Mikaela was in awe at the tiaras in each box.

"I'm a princess, Daddy!" Alyssa said so excitedly that he thought she was about to cry.

He kissed her head. "Yes, you are. Both of you."

"I'm the winner of a beauty pageant," Mikaela said, taking a spin, then struck a pose.

It took a lot of coaxing, but finally Marlon was

able to calm them down so they could get ready for church.

Their baths didn't damper their excitement. "Is Ms. Portia coming with us?" Mikaela's expression hopeful.

He shook his head sadly. "She has to work today." After praying this morning, he'd texted her, Merry Christmas, my lovely.

Merry Christmas and Happy Birthday to Jesus, handsome.

He had grinned at the endearment. I miss you.

Miss you more. Got to go.

"But it's Christmas," Mikaela said, frowning and bringing him back to the present.

"I know." Marlon would suffer her absence all day.

"You've got her a present, right?" Mikaela turned around, so he could zip up the white dress his mother had bought for Christmas, and a matching dress for Alyssa who stood at attention to be next.

He chuckled at his daughter's reminder, as if he needed one. "I sure do, baby."

"Let's take it to her now?" his daughter insisted.

"Maybe we will, later. We have to celebrate Jesus this Christmas morning at church."

"Yay," the girls cheered in unison.

Marlon didn't know if their jubilation was for

Jesus or Portia, but in either case, they were satisfied with his answer. Less than an hour later, they joined his family on the pew. The worship was overpowering as the choir sang a soul-stirring rendition of the "Hallelujah Chorus."

The pastor strolled to the podium, decked out in his festive preaching robe. "Good morning, church, and Merry Christmas. Aren't we celebrating a great day?" He paused. "Whether the world wants to recognize Jesus' birthday or not, He reigns. Isn't it wonderful that God's gifts don't need a tree, but He died on a tree, so we can have His gifts, and we don't have to wait once a year to receive His blessings?"

Many in the congregation shouted, "Amen."

"While we're rejoicing, not everybody knows who Jesus is. The Red Cross' motto is give the gift of life—donate blood. Christ donated His blood on the cross as the gift of eternal life." The pastor's message was brief, but on point. "You can be redeemed. God doesn't take off on holidays. Today would be a great day for your rebirth."

Once the benediction was given and Merry Christmas was exchanged among members, Marlon gathered the girls to do the customary holiday visits.

"Daddy, are we going to give Ms. Portia her gift?" Mikaela asked from the backseat.

"Not yet. We have to stop by Grandma, Uncle

Derek, and Grandpa's houses first."

"Okay." His older daughter pouted, which was comical. Usually, she was hyped about the gifts his parents had bought to dole out to their grandchildren.

"Promise?" Alyssa asked.

"Yep." He was amused how they were concerned whether he had Portia a gift. It was tucked in his jacket pocket. Although Mikaela had prayed for a new mommy, he wondered if she thought Portia was the one. Did she want to be the one for him?

"Grandma, we're going to take Ms. Portia her present," Mikaela stated matter-of-factly, barely clearing the front door at his mother's house.

Lane Washington gave Marlon a teasing smirk. "Really? I guess you'd better hurry and open your presents." Twisting out of their coats, the girls screamed and raced to the living room where gift-wrapped boxes were piled high for them. Once they were alone, she asked, "Is there something you want to give me a heads up about?"

"Nope." Marlon handed her a red envelope. "Merry Christmas." He kissed her cheek, then whistled, amused as he excused himself to follow the girls. His daughters had a workout opening presents, and were ready to devour the food his mother prepared for brunch.

After two helpings of scrambled eggs, pancakes,

French toast, fresh fruit and more, Marlon announced they were leaving for Derek and his dad's house.

"Tell your father and his wife I said Merry Christmas," his mother said. She was no longer bitter over what happened more than twenty years ago, but she put a limit on her cordiality toward him and his third wife. Lane kept her distance.

"I will." As they were on their way out, Derek and his family were coming through the door, their arms were laden with boxes, some for the girls. They were saving him a trip to their house.

"Hey, brother-in-law, we were trying to catch you before you left," Robyn said. "Here are our presents."

The girls went through a second round of gifts opening while Marlon retrieved Derek, Robyn, and their children's their gifts from the car. About an hour later, he checked his watch and attempted to leave again. Alyssa wasn't ready, but Mikaela was more than eager. She whispered something in his baby daughter's ear and it sparked her to get her coat and beat them to the door.

Across town, he ushered his daughters into Tyrone Washington's house with the tokens they had purchased for their grandpa and granny—what they called his wife. Once again, Mikaela announced they were going to take Ms. Portia her gift.

While the girls opened their gifts, his dad sat next to him. "Are you sure about Portia? I haven't met her, you know."

The accusation wasn't lost on Marlon. "You will." He told his father where she worked and what she did.

Tyrone bobbed his head. "The girls seem to really like her."

"They love her," Marlon corrected.

"What about you? Are you with her for their sake, or is she someone you can see yourself with down the road?"

"I have no doubt she's the missing piece in my heart." He turned away from watching the girls and met his father's concerned look. "I love her, too— very much—so no, I'm not settling." *Like you have*, he kept to himself.

His father physically relaxed. To say his father was a tortured soul from his life choices was an understatement. When he recovered from the errors of his ways, Tyrone drilled into Derek and Marlon's heads after their divorces not to settle as he had done with Janice. Derek's remarriage to Robyn, brought tears to their father's eyes.

Marlon checked the time. One thing he had learned about Portia' job was never to contact her leading up to the newscast because it was crunch time. The news would air in forty minutes.

Even though he had her gift, he wondered if he needed to bring her a plate. Taking a chance, he texted her. `Hungry? The girls and I can bring you something to eat.`

`No need. The station catered dinner,` she texted back almost immediately.

`Can you have visitors?`

`Yes.`

Marlon and his dad chatted until it was time to go. Mikaela had her coat on before he did and was already helping Alyssa with hers. Half an hour later, he parked in front of the studios of KSMT-TV. Marlon had never been inside a television station. After signing the guest log, they waited. Portia appeared minutes later dressed in casual attire—a sweater, jeans, and ankle boots—that only enhanced her beauty.

"Merry Christmas," the girls shouted and raced toward her. Their tiaras, they had begged him to let them wear, dangled in their hair with every step. Portia *ahh*ed and *ooh*ed, doting on them so much, Marlon wondered if she had forgotten about him.

Slipping his hands into his pants pockets, he rocked on his heels, then cleared his throat. She glanced up, then gave him her full attention. "Hey."

"Merry Christmas, beautiful. You should be

wearing a crown too."

Alyssa nodded and reached for Portia's hand, Mikaela snatched the other one, so that left Marlon to trail them as she escorted them inside the newsroom. He commented how quiet the place was during a brief tour she gave them.

"Because it's a holiday," she explained. "There's only a skeleton crew, since most people are off."

The tour ended at Portia's temporary workstation, and Marlon retrieved her gift from inside his jacket.

Mikaela frowned when she eyed the long narrow box. "Daddy, that's too big for a ring." Mikaela twisted her lips in disappointment.

The surprise on Portia's face matched his. Mikaela knew too much about grown folks' conversations. Before he could remind her about her manners, she chatted away, "Ms. Portia, you do like little girls, don't you?"

"Of course, especially you and your sister."

Her declaration seemed to make his daughter's day as she hugged Portia tight, as if she wasn't going to let her go. Alyssa did the same. Jutting her chin, Mikaela gave him with a "See, I told you so," look.

What in the world was going on in his oldest daughter's head? he wondered. Portia wouldn't meet his eyes, so he had no idea what she was thinking.

Getting to her feet, she thanked him for her gift, then announced she had to get back to work and prepare for the night's newscast. Her crestfallen expression revealed she didn't want them to go as she strolled beside them, retracing their steps to the lobby. Where his daughters were distracted by the large decorated tree.

Portia slowed her step and faced him. "I didn't know we were going to exchange gifts today, but I do have one present that I didn't leave at home."

"Okay." Marlon stared, waiting. Was it hidden in the lobby? He lifted a brow as she leaned close to his ear.

"I love you too. Merry Christmas." Stepping back, her lips curled upward in a seductive tease.

His attempt at regulating his racing heart failed. His heart thumped wildly in his chest. He opened his mouth and spoke very slowly. "*Umm-hmm.* I want that gift-wrapped, Ms. Hunter." With Mikaela watching them, Marlon reluctantly bid her good night. They definitely would have a long, long talk.

Tears streamed down Mikaela's cheeks when she knelt to thank God for all her gifts. "Jesus, where's my mommy for Christmas?"

"Lights off, my lovely daughter."

Mikaela sniffed, and her voice shook. She tried

to blink back the tears as she looked at her father. "Daddy, I'm sorry about what I said earlier to Ms. Portia. You mad at me?"

"Hey, hey." He frowned, coming into her room and sitting on her bed. Her father pulled her off the floor into his lap, and she cried more. She liked when he rocked her whenever she was sad.

"I'm not mad at you," he said, kissing the top of her head, "but you're not supposed to interrupt when I'm talking, remember?"

She bobbed her head and sniffed. "But I prayed...*hiccup*...and asked Jesus for a mommy for Christmas...*hiccup*...and you didn't ask Ms. Portia to be our mommy." She couldn't stop crying.

"Baby...*shhh*." He rocked her. "God heard your prayers. Now, we have to wait on God's perfect timing, not ours, okay? You keep praying."

She nodded, then he rubbed sloppy kisses on her cheeks until she giggled. "Stop."

"It's been a good Christmas. You need to get your sleep so you can become more beautiful every day."

"Like Ms. Portia?"

He laughed. "Yes." Instead of turning off the light, he began to sing.

She drifted off to sleep, enjoying the sound of her daddy's deep voice.

EPILOGUE

Weeks later...

In the middle of Wal-Mart, Portia got the call. The station offered her a full-time position, making more money than she had in Kansas City. God had answered her prayer. Once she relayed the news to Marlon who was beside her, she had bawled in his arms, tears of joy.

"Ah, my damsel in distress," he whispered, brushing kisses in her hair.

Sniffing, she looked at him and frowned. "Huh?"

"Nothing, babe." He grinned. "I think we should celebrate."

And they did a week later. The celebration would replace the craziness that her birthday had brought for the past couple of years—served divorce papers, then the dissolution granted. Those had been some dark days. Not tonight, she was too giddy to be sad about anything, even the chipped nail after her pricey manicure.

"I'm happy you're making new memories," Coy said, hugging her after appraising her outfit for the dinner date. A pearl necklace accented her little black dress, which draped her curves. She had even splurged on a hair appointment and other pampering.

"What about my big sister? You still don't

believe in a second chance at love?" Portia smiled.

"Maybe a little after watching you and Mr. Washington." Coy measured a small space between her thumb and finger. When the doorbell rang, she hurried away. "Saved by the bell."

After a final scrutiny in the mirror, Portia inhaled and exhaled slowly.

Weeping may endure for a night, but My joy comes in the morning. God whispered Psalm 30:5

The Scripture almost made her cry. God's Word was true. Stepping out of the bathroom, she turned toward the living room and froze. He was talking to Emerald and Coy, then paused mid-sentence and glanced in her direction as if her fragrance tickled his senses. "Wow."

Dismissing his audience, he pivot, and his steps seemed calculated until he towered over her. His eyes sparkled. "Wow," he repeated and gathered her in his arms to deliver the hug she craved at his greeting. "Ready, Ms. Hunter?" His husky voice made her shiver.

"Been ready, birthday man." She nodded as Coy shoved her coat in her arms. Emerald hooked her purse on the other arm as if she was a mannequin. Moments later, she was in Marlon's car and he was reaching for her hand.

Portia didn't ask where he was taking her. It didn't matter as long as he was near to protect her from the demons that wanted to remind her of a tormented love from the wrong man.

There is no fear in love. Perfect love casts out fear: because fear hath torment. God whispered 1 John 4:18.

Portia smiled to herself. She felt God's unconditional love and Marlon's. Closing her eyes, she relaxed and enjoyed the ride.

Although their suburban community of Kirkwood offered a variety of fine dining and café eateries, they had seldom frequented any. Marlon liked to drive. In St. Louis, a motorist could get to most places in plus or minus thirty minutes. He had chosen Elaia in the Tower Grove area of South St. Louis City.

Marlon was an authentic romantic at heart—telling her he loved her for the first time during a snowfall, feeding her when she was sick, and giving her a two-hundred-dollar gift card—that blew her mind!

I charge you to find and remember the good in people. I will judge the bad, God whispered.

Portia swallowed. What bad? she mused. Marlon was as perfect as a godly man could be, blemishes and all, she loved him.

Once they entered Elaia, the ambiance impressed Portia. The colorful decor and light oak wood floors were inviting. Brick fireplaces and thick wood carvings, which had been preserved from the original builders, made her feel at home.

Seated almost immediately, their server approached the table as Marlon linked his fingers through hers. She sucked in her breath at his touch. She felt cherished.

"Are we celebrating a special occasion?" their server asked.

"Occasions," Marlon answered. "Our birthdays, a new job of sorts, a new year, and new beginnings."

"Excellent." The dark-haired, clean-cut man beamed, then proceeded to tell them the specials.

Portia covered her giggles while Marlon placed their orders as if he was trying to get rid of the guy.

Clearing his throat, Marlon gave her his undivided attention. "You know I love you more than I have ever loved another woman. Yes, I was married before, but as I began to reflect on my feelings for you, I separated my attraction from love. I'm deeply attracted and hopelessly in love with you."

Her vision blurred, and her heart fluttered at his heartfelt words. Then he fingered the exquisite charm bracelet that had been the Christmas present Mikaela wasn't happy with. Since then, this jewelry had become a piece of her daily attire. Her birthstone, his and the girls' birthstones and another charm with the inscription "You are loved" dangled from her wrist.

"I love this...and you." Portia tilted her head and admired his handsomeness. There was more to Marlon Washington than looks. "You make me smile."

Unwittingly, she sparked a game of tit-for-tat about each other's attributes during their four-course meal. Once they finished, the server presented a complimentary slice of cheesecake for them to share in honor of their birthdays. Marlon fed her, and she returned the favor until the dessert was gone.

"This was nice. Now I have new memories." Last year at this time, Portia hoped to find happiness again. She just didn't know the when, where, and who until now.

Faith is the substance of things hoped for, the evidence of things not seen, God whispered Hebrews 11:1.

"I've got one more." He reached in his pocket and pulled out a small box. She swallowed, watching him toy with it and her emotions.

Marlon flipped open the lid and acted as if he was studying the diamond that sparkled as light from the wall sconces bounced off of it. "I happened to walk into this jewelry store." He shrugged. "And I just happened to see this and thought of you." The man knew how to draw her into a trance, and she couldn't blink. "I'd get down on one knee and propose if I thought you would say yes. My heart's been broken too, babe, but God has mended me."

Closing her eyes, she let his words soak in. There was no pretense with this man. Opening them, she smirked. "Why don't you try and see?"

"Woman, don't play with me." He pushed back his chair and knelt. When he looked up, it was as if she could see his soul. "Portia Hunter, our past regrets are in the past. I believe we can build a better future together than apart. Let's love each other back to the life God had for us all along. Will you marry me?"

"Yes," she whispered without hesitation. Tears sprung from deep within until she was bawling. Marlon pulled her from her seat and held until she slowly composed herself. Once she quieted, he took her face in his hands and kissed her until they both needed to breathe.

"Sorry I fell apart," she said, embarrassed, shaking her head.

"God has given me the strength to catch you if you fall."

I said yes, dabbing at her eyes. "When should we tell the girls?"

"Now, if you're ready to go." Marlon settled the bill and took the scenic route to his mother's house.

They arrived and shared a short but sweet kiss, then using his key, they entered the house. His mother was dozing in a chair while Alyssa was reading and Mikaela was watching a kid-friendly sitcom rerun. His daughter glanced over her shoulder, then leaped to her feet.

"Daddy, Ms. Portia." She bypassed Marlon and came to her. Alyssa dropped her book. His mother woke, folded her hands, and watched them.

"God has answered your prayers," Marlon said, causing Portia to wonder what had been Mikaela's prayer. Then she knew when he added, "He's giving you a new mommy."

Mikaela's expression was priceless as the words seemed to register. "Hi, Mommy!" she screamed.

Portia's heart melted at the endearment. "Hi, my beautiful daughter."

Tears streamed down Mikaela's cheeks and she lifted her arms, praising God. Alyssa mimicked her. In a blink of an eye, the power of the Holy Ghost fell upon Mikaela, and heavenly tongues flowed out of her mouth as she continued to worship the Lord.

Portia sniffed. "Oh, I'm so looking forward to being a wife and mother in this family." So many prayers mad been answered.

Book Club Discussion

1. Talk about Mikaela's prayer for a mommy and her disappointment with her father's gift to Portia.

2. Despite her heartache, Portia was willing to give love a second chance, but Coy wasn't. What do you think was holding Coy back?

3. God granted Mikaela's prayer, but it was in His timing. Discuss how we put a timeframe on God and then react when He doesn't come through on our deadline.

4. What was the turning point in Marlon and Portia's lives that brought them together in a relationship?

5. Talk about Mikaela's prayer for a mommy and her disappointment with her father's gift to Portia.

6. What prayers are you waiting for God to answer today? His timing is perfect, and His Word won't return to Him void.

Thanks for reading Book 2 of Gifts from God series. If you enjoyed the story, please post an honest review, and visit my website at:

www.patsimmons.net.

Thanks in advance. I hope you will try my other holiday titles.

AUTHOR'S NOTE

Pat Simmons has celebrated ten years as a published author with more than thirty titles. She is a self-proclaimed genealogy sleuth who is passionate about researching her ancestors and then casting them in starring roles in her novels.

She is a three-time recipient of the Romance Slam Jam Emma Rodgers Award for Best Inspirational Romance. Pat describes the evidence of the gift of the Holy Ghost as an amazing, unforgettable, life-altering experience.

Pat holds a B.S. in mass communications from Emerson College in Boston, Massachusetts. She has worked in various media positions for more than twenty years. Currently, she oversees the media publicity for the annual RT Booklovers Conventions.

She has been a featured speaker and workshop presenter at various venues across the country and converted her sofa-strapped sports fanatic husband into an amateur travel agent, untrained bodyguard, GPS-guided chauffeur.

Readers may learn more about Pat and her books by connecting with her on social media, www.patsimmons.net, or by contacting her at authorpatsimmons@gmail.

OTHER CHRISTIAN TITLES

The Guilty Jamieson Legacy series

Book I: *Guilty of Love*

Book II: *Not Guilty of Love*

Book III: *Still Guilty*

Book IV: *The Acquittal*

Book V: *Guilty by Association*

Book VI: *The Guilt Trip*

Book VII: *Free from Guilt*

Book VIII: *The Confession*

The Carmen Sisters

Book I: *No Easy Catch*

Book II: *In Defense of Love*

Book III: *Driven to Be Loved*

Book IV: *Redeeming Heart*

Love at the Crossroads

Book I: *Stopping Traffic*

Book II: *A Baby for Christmas*

Book III: *The Keepsake*

Book IV: *What God Has for Me*

Book V: *Every Woman Needs a Praying Man*

Making Love Work Anthology

Book I: *Love at Work*
Book II: *Words of Love*
Book III: *A Mother's Love*

Restore My Soul series

Crowning Glory
Jet: The Back Story
Love Led by the Spirit

Perfect Chance at Love series:

Love by Delivery
Late Summer Love

Gifts from God

Couple by Christmas
Prayers Answered by Christmas

Single titles

Talk to Me
Her Dress (novella)
Christmas Greetings
Prayers Answered by Christmas

Anderson Brothers series

Book I: Love for the Holidays (Three novellas):
A Christian Christmas, A Christian Easter, and A Christian Father's Day

Book II: *A Woman After David's Heart (Valentine's Day)*

Book III: *A Noelle for Nathan* (Book 3 of the Andersen Brothers)

In *Love by Delivery*, Senior Accounts Manager Dominique Hayes has it all money, a car and a condo. Well, almost. She's starting to believe love has passed her by. One thing for sure, she can't hurry God, so she continues to wait while losing hope that a special Godly man will ever make his appearance. Package Courier Ashton Taylor knows a man who finds a wife finds a good thing. The only thing standing in his way of finding the right woman is his long work hours. Or maybe not. A chance meeting changes everything. When love finally comes knocking, will Dominique open the door and accept Ashton's special delivery?

In *Late Summer Love*, it takes strategies to win a war, but prayer and spiritual intervention are needed to win a godly woman's heart. God has been calling out to Blake Cross ever since Blake was deployed in Iraq and he took his safety for granted. Now, back on American soil, Blake still won't surrender his soul--until he meets Paige Blake during a family reunion. When the Lord gives Blake an ultimatum, is Blake listening, and is he finally ready to learn what it takes to be a godly man fit for a godly woman?

In *Crowning Glory,* Book 1, Cinderella had a prince; Karyn Wallace has a King. While Karyn served four years in prison for an unthinkable crime, she embraced salvation through Crowns for Christ outreach ministry. After her release, Karyn stays strong and confident, despite the stigma society places on ex-offenders. Since Christ strengthens the underdog, Karyn refuses to sway away from the scripture, "He who the Son has set free is free indeed." Levi Tolliver, for the most part, is a practicing Christian. One contradiction is he doesn't believe in turning the other cheek. He's steadfast there is a price to pay for every sin committed, especially after the untimely death of his wife during a robbery. Then Karyn enters Levi's life. He is enthralled not only with her beauty, but her sweet spirit until he learns about her incarceration. If Levi can accept that Christ paid Karyn's debt in full, then a treasure awaits him. This is a powerful tale and reminds readers of the permanency of redemption.

Jet: The Back Story to Love Led By the Spirit, Book 2, to say Jesetta "Jet" Hutchens has issues is an understatement. In *Crowning Glory,* Book 1 of the Restoring My Soul series, she releases a firestorm of anger with an unforgiving heart. But every hurting soul has a history. In *Jet: The Back Story to Love Led by the*

Spirit, Jet doesn't know how to cope with the loss of her younger sister, Diane.

But God sets her on the road to a spiritual recovery. To make sure she doesn't get lost, Jesus sends the handsome and single Minister Rossi Tolliver to be her guide.

Psalm 147:3 says Jesus can heal the brokenhearted and bind up their wounds. That sets the stage for *Love Led by the Spirit.*

In *Love Led by the Spirit,* Book 3, Minister Rossi Tolliver is ready to settle down. Besides the outwardly attraction, he desires a woman who is sweet, humble, and loves church folks. Sounds simple enough on paper, but when he gets off his knees, praying for that special someone to come into his life, God opens his eyes to the woman who has been there all along. There is only a slight problem. Love is the farthest thing from Jesetta "Jet" Hutchens' mind. But Rossi, the man and the minister, is hard to resist. Is Jet ready to allow the Holy Spirit to lead her to love?

In *Stopping Traffic,* Book 1, Candace Clark has a phobia about crossing the street, and for good reason. As fate would have it, her daughter's principal assigns her to crossing guard duties as part of the school's Parent Participation program. With no choice in the matter, Candace begrudgingly accepts her stop sign and safety vest, then reports to her designated crosswalk. Once Candace is determined to overcome her fears, God opens the door for a blessing, and Royce Kavanaugh enters into her life, a firefighter built to rescue any damsel in distress. When a spark of attraction ignites, Candace and Royce soon discover there's more than one way to stop traffic.

In *A Baby for Christmas*, Book 2, yes, diamonds are a girl's best friend, but in Solae Wyatt-Palmer's case, she desires something more valuable. Captain Hershel Kavanaugh is a divorcee and the father of two adorable little boys. Solae has never been married and longs to be a mother. Although Hershel showers her with expensive gifts, his hesitation about proposing causes Solae to walk and never look back. As the holidays approach, Hershel must convince Solae that she has everything he could ever want for Christmas.

In *The Keepsake*, Book 3, Until death us do part…or until Desiree walks away. Desiree "Desi" Bishop is devastated when she finds evidence of her husband's affair. God knew she didn't get married only to one day have to stand before a judge and file for a divorce. But Desi wants out no matter how much her heart says to forgive Michael. That isn't easier said than done. She sees God's one acceptable reason for a divorce as the only opt-out clause in her marriage. Michael Bishop is a repenting man who loves his wife of three years. If only...he had paid attention to the red flags God sent to keep him from falling into the devil's snares. But Michael didn't and he had fallen. Although God had forgiven him instantly when he repented, Desi's forgiveness is moving at a snail's pace. In the end, after all the tears have been shed and forgiveness granted and received, the couple learns that some marriages are worth keeping

In *What God Has for Me*, Book 4, Halcyon Holland is leaving her live-in boyfriend, taking their daughter and the baby in her belly with her. She's tired of waiting for the ring, so she buys herself one. When her ex doesn't reconcile their relationship, Halcyon begins to second-guess whether or not she compromised her chance for a happily ever after. After all, what man in his right mind would want to deal with the community stigma of 'baby mama drama?' But Zachary Bishop has had his eye on Halcyon since the first time he saw her. Without a ring on her finger, Zachary prays that she will come to her senses and not only leave Scott, but come back to God. What one man doesn't cherish, Zach is ready to treasure. Not deterred by Halcyon's broken spirit, Zachary is on a mission to offer her a second chance at love that she can't refuse. And as far as her adorable children are concerned, Zachary's love is unconditional for a ready-made family.

Halcyon will soon learn that her past circumstances won't hinder the Lord's blessings because what God has for her, is for her…and him…and the children.

In *Every Woman Needs a Praying Man*, Book 5, first impressions can make or break a business deal and they definitely could be a relationship buster, but an ill-timed panic attack draws two strangers together. Unlike firefighters who run into danger, instincts tell businessman Tyson Graham to head the other way as fast as he can when he meets a certain damsel in distress. Days later, the same woman struts through his door for a job interview. Monica Wyatt might possess the outward beauty and the brains on paper, but Tyson doesn't trust her to work for his firm, or maybe he doesn't trust his heart around her.

In *A Christian Christmas*, Book 1, Christian's Christmas will never be the same for Joy Knight if Christian Andersen has his way. Not to be confused with a secret Santa, Christian and his family are busier than Santa's elves making sure the Lord's blessings are distributed to those less fortunate by Christmas day. Joy is playing the hand that life dealt her, rearing four children in a home that is on the brink of foreclosure. She's not looking for a handout, but when Christian rescues her in the checkout line; her niece thinks Christian is an angel. Joy thinks he's just another man who will eventually leave, disappointing her and the children. Although Christian is a servant of the Lord, he is a flesh and blood man and all he wants for Christmas is Joy Knight. Can time spent with Christian turn Joy's attention from her financial woes to the real meaning of Christmas—and true love?

In *A Christian Easter*, how to celebrate Easter becomes a balancing act for Christian and Joy Andersen and their four children. Chocolate bunnies, colorful stuffed baskets, and flashy fashion shows are their competition. Despite the enticements, Christian refuses to succumb without a fight. And it becomes a tug of war when his recently adopted ten-year-old daughter, Bethani, wants to participate in her friend's Easter tradition. Christian hopes he has instilled Proverbs 22:6, into the children's heart in the short time of being their dad.

In *A Christian Father's Day,* three fathers, one Father's Day and four children. Will the real dad, please stand up. It's never too late to be a father—or is it? Christian Andersen was looking forward to spending his first Father's Day with his adopted children---all four of them. But Father's day becomes more complicated than Christian or Joy ever imagined. Christian finds himself faced with living up to his name when things don't go his way to enjoy an idyllic once a year celebration. But he depends on God to guide him through the journey.

(All three of Christian's individual stories are in the Love for the Holidays anthology (Book 1 of the Andersen Brothers series)

In *A Woman After David's Heart,* Book 2, David Andersen doesn't have a problem indulging in Valentine's Day, per se, but not on a first date. Considering it was the love fest of the year, he didn't want a woman to get any ideas that a wedding ring was forthcoming before he got a chance to know her. So he has no choice but to wait until the whole Valentine's Day hoopla was over, then he would make his move on a sister in his church he can't take his eyes off of. For the past two years and counting, Valerie Hart hasn't been the recipient of a romantic Valentine's Day dinner invitation. To fill the void, Valerie keeps herself busy with God's business, hoping the Lord will send her perfect mate soon. Unfortunately, with no prospects in sight, it looks like that won't happen again this year. A Woman After David's Heart is a Valentine romance novella that can be enjoyed with or without a box of chocolates.

In *A Noelle for Nathan,* Book 3, is a story of kindness, selflessness, and falling in love during the Christmas season. Andersen Investors & Consultants, LLC, CFO Nathan Andersen (A Christian Christmas) isn't looking for attention when he buys a homeless man a meal, but grade school teacher Noelle Foster is watching his every move with admiration. His generosity makes him a man after her own heart. While donors give more to children and families in need around the holiday season, Noelle Foster believes in giving year-round after seeing many of her students struggle with hunger and finding a warm bed at night. At a second-chance meeting, sparks fly when Noelle and Nathan share a kindred spirit with their passion to help those less fortunate. Whether they're doing charity work or attending Christmas parties, the couple becomes inseparable. Although Noelle and Nathan exchange gifts, the biggest present is the one from Christ.

MAKING LOVE WORK SERIES

This series can be read in any order.

In *A Mother's Love,* to Jillian Carter, it's bad when her own daughter beats her to the altar. She became a teenage mother when she confused love for lust one summer. Despite the sins of her past, Jesus forgave her and blessed her to be the best Christian example for Shana. Jillian is not looking forward to becoming an empty-nester at thirty-nine. The old adage, she's not losing a daughter, but gaining a son-in-law is not comforting as she braces for a lonely life ahead. What she doesn't expect is for two men to vie for her affections: Shana's biological father who breezes back into their lives as a redeemed man and practicing Christian. Not only is Alex still good looking, but he's willing to right the wrong he's done in the past. Not if Dr. Dexter Harris has anything to say about it. The widower father of the groom has set his sights on Jillian and he's willing to pull out all the stops to woo her. Now the choice is hers. Who will be the next mother's love?

In *Love at Work,* how do two people go undercover to hide an office romance in a busy television newsroom? In plain sight, of course. Desiree King is an assignment editor at KDPX-TV in St. Louis, MO. She dispatches a team to wherever breaking news happens. Her focus is to stay ahead of the competition. Overall, she's easy-going, respectable, and compassionate. But when it comes to dating a fellow coworker, she refuses to cross that professional line. Award-winning investigative reporter Bryan Mitchell makes life challenging for Desiree with his thoughtful gestures, sweet notes, and support. He tries to convince Desiree that as Christians, they could show coworkers how to blend their personal and private lives without compromising their morals.

In *Words of Love,* call it old fashion, but Simone French was smitten with a love letter. Not a text, email, or Facebook post, but a love letter sent through snail mail. The prose wasn't the corny roses-are-red-and-violets-are-blue stuff. The first letter contained short accolades for a job well done. Soon after, the missives were filled with passionate words from a man who confessed the hidden secrets of his soul. He revealed his unspoken weaknesses, listed his uncompromising desires, and unapologetically noted his subtle strengths. Yes, Rice Taylor was ready to surrender to love. *Whew.* Closing her eyes, Simone inhaled the faint lingering smell of roses on the beige plain stationery. She had a testimony. If anyone would listen, she would proclaim that love was truly blind.

Pat Simmons

SINGLE TITLES

WWW.PATSIMMONS.NET

In *Talk to Me,* despite being deaf as a result of a fireworks explosion, CEO of a St. Louis non-profit company, Noel Richardson, expertly navigates the hearing world. What some view as a disability, Noel views as a challenge—his lack of hearing has never held him back. It also helps that he has great looks, numerous university degrees, and full bank accounts. But those assets don't define him as a man who longs for the right woman in his life. Deciding to visit a church service, Noel is blindsided by the most beautiful and graceful Deaf interpreter he's ever seen. Mackenzie Norton challenges him on every level through words and signing, but as their love grows, their faith is tested. When their church holds a yearly revival, they witness the healing power of God in others. Mackenzie has faith to believe that Noel can also get in on the blessing. Since faith comes by hearing, whose voice does Noel hear in his heart, Mackenzie or God's?

TESTIMONY: *If I Should Die Before I Wake.*

It is of the LORD's mercies that we are not consumed because His compassions fail not. They are new every morning, great is Thy faithfulness. Lamentations 3:22-23, God's mercies are sure; His promises are fulfilled, but a dawn of a new morning is God' grace. If you need a testimony about God's grace, then If I Should Die Before I Wake will encourage your soul. Nothing happens in our lives by chance. If you need a miracle, God's got that too. Trust Him. Has it been a while since you've had a testimony? Increase your prayer life, build your faith and walk in victory because, without a test, there is no testimony. (eBook only)

In *Her Dress*, sometimes a woman just wants to splurge on something new, especially when she's about to attend an event with movers and shakers. Find out what happens when Pepper Trudeau is all dressed up and goes to the ball, but another woman is modeling the same attire. At first, Pepper is embarrassed, then the night gets interesting when she meets Drake Logan. *Her Dress* is a romantic novella about the all too common occurrence— two women shopping at the same place. Maybe having the same taste isn't all bad. Sometimes a good dress is all you need to meet the man of your dreams. (eBook only)

In *Christmas Greetings*, Saige Carter loves everything about Christmas: the shopping, the food, the lights, and of course, Christmas wouldn't be complete without family and friends to share in the traditions they've created together. Plus, Saige is extra excited about her line of Christmas greeting cards hitting store shelves, but when she gets devastating news around the holidays, she wonders if she'll ever look at Christmas the same again. Daniel Washington is no Scrooge, but he'd rather skip the holidays altogether than spend them with his estranged family. After one too many arguments around the dinner table one year, Daniel had enough and walked away from the drama. As one year has turned into many, no one seems willing to take the first step toward reconciliation. When Daniel reads one of Saige's greeting cards, he's unsure if the words inside are enough to erase the pain and bring about forgiveness. Once God reveals to them His purpose for their lives, they will have a reason to rejoice.

In *Couple by Christmas*, holidays haven't been the same for Derek Washington since his divorce. He and his ex-wife, Robyn, go out the way to avoid each other. This Christmas may be different when he decides to gives his son, Tyler, the family he once had before the split.

Derek's going to need the Lord's intervention to soften his ex-wife's heart to agree. God's help doesn't come in the way he expected, but it's all good because everything falls in place for them to be a couple by Christmas.

In *Guilty of Love,* when do you know the most important decision of your life is the right one? Reaping the seeds from what she's sown; Cheney Reynolds moves into a historic neighborhood in Ferguson, Missouri, and becomes reclusive. Her first neighbor, the incomparable Mrs. Beatrice Tilley Beacon aka Grandma BB, is an opinionated childless widow. Grandma BB is a self-proclaimed expert on topics Cheney isn't seeking advice—everything from landscaping to hip-hop dancing to romance. Then there is Parke Kokumuo Jamison VI, a direct descendant of a royal African tribe. He learned his family ancestry, African history, and lineage preservation before he could count. Unwittingly, they are drawn to each other, but it takes Christ to weave their lives into a spiritual bliss while He exonerates their past indiscretions.

In *Not Guilty,* one man, one woman, one God and one big problem. Malcolm Jamieson wasn't the man who got away, but the man God instructed Hallison Dinkins to set free. Instead of their explosive love affair leading them to the wedding altar, God diverted Hallison to the prayer altar during her first visit back to church in years. Malcolm was convinced that his woman had lost her mind to break off their engagement. Didn't Hallison know that Malcolm, a tenth generation descendant of a royal

African tribe, couldn't be replaced? Once Malcolm concedes that their relationship can't be salvaged, he issues Hallison his own edict, "If we're meant to be with each other, we'll find our way back. If not, that means that there's a love stronger than what we had." His words begin to haunt Hallison until she begins to regret their break up, and that's where their story begins. Someone has to retreat, and God never loses a battle.

In *Still Guilty,* Cheney Reynolds Jamieson made a choice years ago that is now shaping her future and the future of the men she loves. A botched abortion left her unable to carry a baby to term, and her husband, Parke K. Jamison VI, is expected to produce heirs. With a wife who cannot give him a child, Parke vows to find and get custody of his illegitimate son by any means necessary. Meanwhile, Cheney's twin brother, Rainey, struggles with his anger over his ex-girlfriend's actions that haunt him, and their father, Dr. Roland Reynolds, fights to keep an old secret in the past.

In *The Acquittal*, two worlds apart, but their hearts dance to the same African drum beat. On a professional level, Dr. Rainey Reynolds is a competent, highly sought-after orthodontist. Inwardly, he needs to be set free from the chaos of revelations that make him question if happiness is obtainable. To get away from the drama, Rainey is willing to leave the country under the guise of a mission trip with Dentist Without Borders. Will changing his surroundings really change him? If one woman can heal his wounds, then he will believe that there is really peace after the storm.

Ghanaian beauty Josephine Abena Yaa Amoah returns to Africa after completing her studies as an exchange student in St. Louis, Missouri. Although her heart bleeds for his peace, she knows she must step back and pray for Rainey's surrender to Christ in order for God to acquit him of his self-inflicted mental torture. In the Motherland of Ghana, Africa, Rainey visits the places of his ancestors but will he embrace the liberty that Christ's Blood really does set every man free.

In *Guilty by Association,* how important is a name? To the St. Louis Jamiesons who are tenth generation descendants of a royal African tribe—everything. To the Boston Jamiesons whose father never married their mother—there is no loyalty or legacy. Kidd Jamieson suffers from the "angry" male syndrome because of his father absentee but insisted his two sons carry his last name. It takes an old woman who mingles genealogy truths and Bible verses together for Kidd to realize his worth as a strong black man. He learns it's not his association with the name that identifies him, but the man he becomes that defines him.

In *The Guilt Trip,* Aaron "Ace" Jamieson is living a carefree life. He's good-looking, respectable when he's in the mood, but his weakness is women. If a woman tries to ambush him with a pregnancy, he takes off in the other direction. It's a lesson learned from his absentee father that responsibility is optional. Talise Rogers has a bright future ahead of her. She's pretty and has no problem catching a man's eye, which is exactly what she does with Ace. Trapping Ace Jamieson is the furthest thing from

Taleigh's mind when she learns she is pregnant and Ace rejects her. "I want nothing from you Ace, not even your name." And Talise meant it.

In *Free From Guilt*, it's salvation round-up time and Cameron Jamieson's name is on God's hit list. Although his brothers and cousins embraced God—thanks to the women in their lives—the two-degreed MIT graduate isn't going to let any woman take him down that path without a fight. He's satisfied with his career, social calendar, and good genes. But God uses a beautiful messenger, Gabrielle Dupree, to show him that he's in a spiritual deficit. Cameron learns the hard way that man's wisdom is like foolishness to God. For every philosophical argument he throws her way, Gabrielle exposes him to scriptures that make him question his worldly knowledge.

In *The Confession,* Sandra Nicholson had made good and bad choices throughout the years, but the best one was to give her life to Christ when her sons were small and to rear them up in the best Christian way she knew how. That was thirty something years ago and Sandra has evolved from a young single mother of two rambunctious boys, Kidd and Ace Jamieson, to a godly woman seasoned with wisdom. Despite the challenges and trials of rearing two strong-willed personalities, Sandra maintained her sanity through the grace of God, which kept gray strands at bay. Now, Sandra Nicholson is on the threshold of happiness, but Kidd believes no man is good enough for his mother, especially if her love interest could be a man just like his absentee father.

THE CARMEN SISTERS SERIES

In *No Easy Catch,* Book 1, Shae Carmen hasn't lost her faith in God, only the men she's come across. Shae's recent heartbreak was discovering that her boyfriend was not only married but on the verge of reconciling with his estranged wife. Humiliated, Shae begins to second guess herself as why she didn't see the signs that he was nothing more than a devil's decoy masquerading as a devout Christian man. St. Louis Outfielder Rahn Maxwell finds himself a victim of an attempted carjacking. The Lord guides him out of harms' way by opening the gunman's eyes to Rahn's identity. The crook instead becomes an infatuated fan and asks for Rahn's autograph, and as a good will gesture, directs Rahn out of the ambush! When the news media gets wind of what happened with the baseball player, Shae's television station lands an exclusive interview. Shae and Rahn's chance meeting sets in motion a relationship where Rahn not only surrenders to Christ but pursues Shae with a purpose to prove that good men are still out there. After letting her guard down, Shae is faced with another scandal that rocks her world. This time the stakes are higher. Not only is her heart on the line, so is her professional credibility. She and Rahn are at odds about how to handle it and friction erupts between them. Will she strike out at love again? The Lord shows Rahn that nothing happens by chance, and everything is done for Him to get the glory.

In Defense of Love, Book 2, lately, nothing in Garrett Nash's life has made sense. When two people close to the U.S. Marshal wrong him deeply, Garrett expects God to remove them from his life. Instead, the Lord relocates Garrett to another city to start over, as if he were the offender instead of the victim.

Criminal attorney Shari Carmen is comfortable in her own skin—most of the time. Being a "dark and lovely" African-American sister has its challenges, especially when it comes to relationships. Although she's a fireball in the courtroom, she knows how to fade into the background and keep the proverbial spotlight off her personal life. But literal spotlights are a different matter altogether.

While playing tenor saxophone at an anniversary party, she grabs the attention of Garrett Nash. And as God draws them closer together, He makes another request of Garrett, one to which it will prove far more difficult to say "Yes, Lord."

In *Redeeming Heart*, Book 3, Landon Thomas (*In Defense of Love*) brings a new definition to the word "prodigal," as in prodigal son, brother or anything else imaginable. It's a good thing that God's love covers a multitude of sins, but He isn't letting Landon off easy. His journey from riches to rags proves to be humbling and a lesson well learned. Real Estate Agent Octavia Winston is a woman on a mission, whether it's God's or hers professionally. One thing is for certain, she's not about to compromise when it comes to a Christian mate, so why did God send a homeless man to steal her heart? Minister Rossi Tolliver (*Crowning Glory*) knows how to minister to God's lost sheep and through God's redemption, the game changes for Landon and Octavia.

In *Driven to Be Loved,* Book 4, on the surface, Brecee Carmen has nothing in common with Adrian Cole. She is a pediatrician certified in trauma care; he is a transportation problem solver for a luxury car dealership (a.k.a., a car salesman). Despite their slow but steady attraction to each other, neither one of them are sure that they're compatible. To complicate matters, Brecee is the sole unattached Carmen when it seems as though everyone else around her—family and friends—are finding love, except her.

Through a series of discoveries, Adrian and Brecee learn that things don't happen by coincidence. Generational forces are at work, keeping promises, protecting family members, and perhaps even drawing Adrian back to the church. For Brecee and Adrian, God has been hard at work, playing matchmaker all along the way for their paths cross at the right time and the right place.

**Check out my fellow Christian fiction authors writing about faith, family, and love. You won't be disappointed! www.blackchristianreads.com

54581133R00113

Made in the USA
Middletown, DE
05 December 2017